I0707598

BROKEN WINDOWS, RENOVATED SOULS

Stories of Emergence

G.E. Russell

G.E. Russell

Copyright © 2023

All Rights Reserved

Dedication

To my wife Stephanie, your love and faith gives me gilded wings.

To my niece, Noellie, your knowledge and demeanor makes the struggle valuable.

I cannot thank you both enough.

G.E. Russell

Acknowledgment

I would like to personally thank and acknowledge everyone at Amazon Publications, particularly Project Coordinator Tina Stone for their remarkable professionalism and support throughout this process.

Table of Contents

About the Author

G. E. Russell is a new author bringing stories of challenges, difficulties, insights, changes and self-discovery in which he hopes to give readers insights into 'threads of commonality' amongst all people. A U.S. Army veteran of the Cold War, G. E. has experienced different cultures and settings which he feels add authenticity and flavor to his works. After serving our country, he attended college to 'primarily play football and have a good time' as he says ('And I was pretty good at both'). Later in life, challenges and events caused him to deeply examine himself and discover a true sense of being; flawed, hopeful, grateful to be living. Returning to college, he graduated cum laude before achieving his Master's Degree from George Washington University College of Law. G. E. enjoyed a highly successful career as an Advanced Practice Paralegal before retiring in 2020. The father of six children, G. E. and his wife currently reside in Arizona.

Neighborhood Watch

"Don't hold dinner for me, I'll be late night tonight."

"Why? What's tonight?"

Loading rolled blueprints under his left armpit, Steve Bankord looked away from his wife Claire, focusing instead on his travel mug and briefcase atop the kitchen island of their suburban home. Claire watched, annoyed but unsurprised.

"Are you going to answer me?" She watched his practiced avoidance. Finally, with hands full, his defensive paraphernalia perimeter built, he replied, "It's a dinner meeting with the Paragon people, and bankers of course." Being Vice-President of Operations at Gilbert and Associates Construction, the largest commercial contractor in Colorado Springs, Steve was constantly tasked with reporting to investors about project completion, operational costs and other matters, right up to ribbon-cutting ceremonies.

Twenty-four years ago, Claire Severson defied her father's expectations and left Wisconsin, going east, hoping to eventually arrive on New York's Madison Avenue. Of average height, slender, a talented swimmer, she still puts in miles twice a week. Now older, a mother, her frame and strength remarkably youthful, her blond hair shorter, an active girl's style, her complexion still clear, showing no lines or layers.

Eighteen years ago, the Monday after graduating from Penn State University, Claire reluctantly came to Colorado with Steve. He suavely assured her their best life was out in the Rockies, a new adventure. A year later they married and honeymooned in Cancun. Two years later, son Bryce was born and Claire submerged into suburban motherhood. Determined not to drown in carpool schedules or part-time cashiering at a local store, she converted the house's fourth bedroom in the southeast corner to a design studio. What good is an MFA in Graphic Design if you're only remembering all you did to get it?

Steve leaned forward, lips puckered, waiting for Claire's reciprocal stretch. Such morning kisses were brief, unexceptional, not much different from any other mechanical, obligatory expressions of love or God forbid, passion. Steve stepped back, set down his briefcase and retrieved his car keys from his jacket pocket.

"Okay, I'll see you later tonight." He turned toward the door, grabbed the worn, oxblood colored valise and stepped away. Claire took her coffee cup to the counter next to the Keurig and began making her next dose. While searching the supply of thimble-shaped plastic caffeine holders, Bryce rounded down the stairs and strode into the kitchen.

"It's just you and me for dinner Bud, anything special you'd like?"

Heading to the refrigerator, he pulled the pitcher of orange juice out. Letting the door shut, he stepped to the cabinet holding drinking glasses. Down onto the counter went the juice as he opened the upper cabinet door.

"Mom, I got baseball and you said I could go to Tanner's after and spend the night, remember?" A glass came down to the counter and pouring commenced. Claire turned from the Keurig and looked to Bryce, "Was that tonight?"

Without looking back, Bryce lifted the glass and tilted his head.A substantial gulp filled his mouth and the glass returned to the counter. He looked to her with wide eyes and tightened lips, his head bobbing as he groaned, "Mmm-mm".

"Oh, I guess I didn't connect today with that plan." She looked out the sink window to the eastern horizon and the valley spreading below. The Keurig was filling her cup as she sensed the world swallowing her. She thought briefly of the work awaiting upstairs and how it no longer challenged her. Five years of lawn and garden equipment catalog layout and artwork can only inspire so much.

Claire built a boutique graphic art and design business during Bryce's lifetime. Her clientele list of thirty-five small to midsize companies, investment firms, medical associations and various manufacturers was lucrative but didn't challenge or excite her creativity or imagination. Three weeks away from her forty-second birthday, life was a social, emotional, professional plateau; a flat horizon for three-hundred-sixty-degrees.

Pulling up his backpack and grabbing a newly crisped Pop-Tart from the toaster, Bryce announced, "Tanner's here, gotta go."

"Okay, listen, call me when you get to Tanner's tonight so I know you're alright. Okay?" A Pop-Tart bite, nod and wink, he bounced down the main hallway and out the front door, "Sure Mom, see ya later."

A blue sky full of the brightest eastern morning sunlight drenched the neighborhood. Claire and Steve bought a two-story house that faced northwest on a small crest on the Rockies front range. Across the street the foothills held a few hiking trails starting at 7200 feet above sea level before rising to somewhere between 9200 and 11,000 feet in elevation. The last house on the street, Timmerman's, was further south from Claire's, lower, closer to the street.

To the other side, also lower in elevation, stood Compton's expansive ranch-style house. Claire's backyard elevation let her see Compton's entire back roof. Steve loved their house sitting on the neighborhood's highest lot. A dog-ear plank fence surrounded Claire's backyard but offered little visual obstruction to the other backyards flowing down the foothills. Standing at the sink, viewing the panorama below her kitchen window, holding her cup with both hands, Claire Bankord dreaded the empty day ahead.

Broken Windows, Renovated Souls

******

The cell phone chirped and vibrated on the artist's table as Claire maneuvered an image on her iMac's screen. The riding lawnmower needed to be smaller to fit in the catalog page. Stopping to commit the image to computer memory, Claire reached over and engaged the phone without checking the caller's identity. Looking out the corner windows of her second-floor studio, she offered, "Hello, this is Claire Bankord.

"Claire, it's Elyse, are you coming to the neighborhood watch committee meeting, tomorrow night?"

Claire blanked, she walked to the southeast window, overlooking the other houses that rambled down to Colorado Springs, "Tomorrow night?"

"Uh-hum, it's important, we need to meet right away." Elyse was in her hyper assertive-modality, singularly focused on getting full compliance from whomever she engaged. Looking across her backyard, beyond her fence, Claire spied something moving behind her neighbor's pine trees. Distracted, Claire asked, "We scheduled a meeting for Friday night?"

"No, we didn't schedule it." Elyse conceded quickly, "I'm calling a special meeting to address a serious problem with one neighbor."

"What's the problem?

"We shouldn't discuss it over the phone, that would violate our transparency policy.All I can say is it's *very* serious, I want everyone present. Can I count on you tomorrow night?"

Elyse's pressure snapped Claire back even though she didn't understand Elyse's urgency, "Well, I suppose."

"Claire, this is important. You're Vice-Chair."There she was; Mrs. Full-Charge, "I need to be sure who's going to attend."

"Okay, Elyse, listen, unless something with Steve or Bryce keeps me, I'll be there.Okay?"

"Okay, good, I'll see you tomorrow night.Seven O'clock, okay? Bye." The click signaled Elyse was onto her next call. Claire stood watching the pine trees down below to the east, curious about what she thought she'd seen. Before she could react, the motion flashed again between the branches, flitting from one tree into the next, left to right, moving toward the open area in the lot corner.

She waited, watching the rhythmic progress of something moving through the widening spaces between the trees until it popped out in broad daylight.Claire's head tweaked back when she saw a man calmly pushing a lawnmower in a smooth, even tempo. Upon reaching the corner eighty-five feet from her window, twenty-four feet below, he smoothly turned about and resumed his pace, eventually disappearing behind the trees that lined his backyard's boundary. Claire's fence defined her eastern lot line and she realized in all her years, this was the first time she ever looked beyond the fence, beyond the trees. She knew across the street from her front door, the mountains stood powerfully. Occasionally, whenever they were outside at the same time, she'd wave to the Compton's. She knew Elyse and husband Nick lived on the other side of Compton's. But why hadn't she looked beyond her backyard, to the northeast and east, before?

The lawn mowing man's house sat on a cul-de-sac, facing east-northeast. A two-story, similar to Claire's, it had a deck and small patio outside the kitchen, facing west. Above one half of the deck, a second deck off the master bedroom, almost completely blocked from view by the Blue Spruce, Aspen and Ponderosa Pine trees that lined the lot's north and western boundaries. But along the southern boundary, to the southeast corner, stood only six-foot high fencing, allowing full illumination under southern and western sunlight.

Claire watched the man return, repeat his pivot and disappear behind the trees again. It was a simple task, one to be repeated frequently during spring and summer, nothing exceptional, a charming diversion from mundane computer screen layout. Looking through her window, Claire let her mind drift into simply observing someone else's physical activity. Then he returned to view, showing only one color in varying tones: he was naked.

Claire's eyes widened as her hand came to her mouth. She watched his every step, his thighs flexing, his arms tanned and muscular, his altogether freedom swinging to and fro in the rhythm of his gait. His face relaxed, wrap-around sunglasses protecting his eyes as he boldly strode about his backyard.

This neighbor, mowing his lawn, this nude man, captivated Claire for fifteen minutes until he finished. He methodically dumped the last load of grass clippings from the mower bag into a plastic garbage can stationed against his southern fence. With a remarkable nonchalance, he brushed clippings off his sweaty body. Once finished with the bag, he turned to the mower and pushed it to the door on the backside of his garage. Leaving the mower there, he walked to his house, behind the trees, out of Claire's sight, leaving her to wonder, '*Who is this guy?*'

Claire worked until almost one-thirty that afternoon, then needed to get outside, away from the catalog. Remembering the naked lawn-mowing man, she decided to go downstairs to her lower level, where sliding glass doors opened to her backyard patio. Over the patio was a larger deck with a staircase down to ground level, much like her neighbor's. But her patio extended southeast creating a large oval-shaped area for the fire pit and chairs. Further along the southern fence, in a space the length of the garage and twelve feet wide, a storage shelter held garden tools, cushions, the lawnmower, trimmer and other suburban landscaping necessities.

Claire walked to the southernmost edge of the fire pit area. Once there she stopped, looked to the southeast where the land descended, flowing back eventually to the fertile prairie of Kansas. After a moment she casually, quietly, turned to view his backyard. Searching beyond the fence, behind the tree's blockade over newly sheared grass to the northwestern corner, she was surprised to see him on his patio, lying on a chaise just off the edge of his deck, still naked.

He reclined in full sunlight, open to the air, the mountains, nature and all things heavenly above. His face relaxed, his arms on each armrest, a small table holding a plastic beverage bottle to one side. Claire was transfixed by a man she'd never seen before. She stood silently, watching his repose, her mind asking, *'Why am I watching this man? What is wrong with me?'*

No answer came, no voice offering a rational explanation, an excuse, outrage, indignation or offense. He was there, lying still, under the sun without a stitch of modesty and even less concern for traditional suburban conduct.

Claire returned to her kitchen hungry, uncertain what to eat. Her mind charged and retreated between convention and curiosity, like fencers thrusting and parrying. She wondered, *'How can he walk around or lay there naked in broad daylight?'*

After a moment, her other inside voice replied, *'He can do what he wants, it's his property. Nobody else's business if he's naked.'*

'What about his neighbors? Their kids?'

Spooning Tuesday leftover casserole onto a paper plate, she defended, *'He's got trees, tall trees and his neighbors all have fences. What kids? They're in school.'*

'But, it's not normal.'

Closing the door, her right hand tapped the digits on the microwave face as she spoke, "Normal. What's normal?"

Pressing 'Start', the microwave's hum sent her back in thought, curious about why someone would mow their lawn naked? Wouldn't they be afraid of something flying out, hitting a sensitive location? She thought about the need to protect one's feet, how foolish it might look mowing naked, except for shoes. And the sunglasses, were his eyes the only part needing protection? What about exposure to ultra-violet and infra-red rays?

As Claire watched the casserole plate rotate in the microwave, her cellphone again jumped with ringtone and vibrations. She pivoted to the counter and looked at the phone, leery that Elyse might return. Seeing 'Gilbert & Assoc' sliding across the screen, Claire was confused.

"Gilbert?" she asked the kitchen. Timidly, she pressed the 'Accept' and 'Speaker' buttons.

"Hello?"

"Uhm, hello, is this Claire?" A voice probed.

"Who are you calling?"

"Uhm, I'm trying to call Claire Bankord, is this her?" The younger female voice cautiously asked.

"Yes, this is Claire Bankord, who's calling please?"

"Uhm, high, this is Ashley, at Gilbert Construction, Steve, I mean, Mr. Bankord, asked me to call you."

"He did? Why?" Claire had never heard of this 'Ashley' person before. Before an answer returned, Claire followed, "Who are you, Ashley?"

"Yeah, I'm Ashley Richardson, Steve's secretary, I mean administrative assistant for Mr. Bankord. He wanted me to see if you'd gotten his dry cleaning yet?"

Standing still, Claire processed the words. Steve never mentioned an administrative assistant before. Curious, Claire asked as the microwave bell dinged, "Dry cleaning? He wants to know if I picked up our dry cleaning?"

"Uhm-hum," Ashley gulped.

Claire shrugged as she took her lunch plate from the warm

cavern, then paused. Her eyes looked to the deck shading the patio outside. Beyond the deck rails, the tops of Blue Spruce, Aspens and Ponderosa's swayed gently in the wind. Entranced, Claire's monotone responded, "Yes, I have it. Why?"

Silence preceded three heavy breaths through the earpiece. Claire listened, before another gulp asked, "You have it. You picked it up already?" A shuffle sound diffused through Claire's phone as she heard a whispered, "She has it."

Another voice, muffled, discernible to Claire spoke and Ashley breathlessly asked, "All of it?"

Nodding to the trees, Claire replied smoothly, "Yes, all of it."

Again, a pause, silence laying on Claire's ears before the breathing on the other end accelerated slightly. Claire waited and listened, taking a bite from her plate, silently chewing, no sound coming through her cellphone. Finally, after swallowing her bite, Claire asked, "Hello, are you there?"

No response: Claire asked again, "Hello?"

Ashley's voice rushed back, a sudden gust, "YES, I'm here. Uhm, okay, I'll tell him, thank you, bye."

The call ended and Claire set her hand down on the counter, mentally examining the conversation, replaying each question and answer. Slowly, methodically, she repeated to herself, 'Have you gotten the dry cleaning yet?'

Broken Windows, Renovated Souls

******

"That'll be thirty-seven sixty-five" the counter-woman announced. Claire produced two twenty-dollar bills and waited for her change. As two dollars and thirty-five cents were placed in her right hand, Claire smiled, then took the multiple plastic-sheathed hangers to her car. For the twelve-minute drive back to her home, Claire mused over this batch's importance, so inauspicious on Monday, now something of interest for Steve and Ashley.

Taking the clothes up to her bedroom, she pulled each hanger out from its shroud; her blouse, her slacks, Steve's three shirts, his slacks and sport coat. Nothing exceptional or curious she thought. She took her blouse, slacks and the shirts into the closet, hanging them on the crossbar. Coming back out, she noticed a small plastic bag hanging inside the neck of the sport coat hanger. Lifting the jacket, a small tag showed a caricatured man and the words, 'We found this in your pocket.'

Claire looked to the bag's contents, something folded, bright, fluorescent pink, having a lacey bric-a-brac design. She lifted the small bag off the hangar and dropped the coat on the bed. Pulling the bag open, her fingers deftly lifted the sheer fabric out before letting the bag fall away. With both hands, she expanded the delicate two-inch wide band of pink, a winding, lace design, stretchable and sheer. As she expanded the fabric from left to right, a triangular piece, attached to one side of the band, dropped at the center, having a single strand of pink fabric connected to the other side. It was a piece of woman's, no, young girl's lingerie, clearly intended for hips never widened by pregnancy.

Claires' awareness focused on the tiny accoutrement, captivated by its unrepentant audacity. Her body wavered ever so slightly as the weight of incredulous discovery surged from her stomach, rising to her throat as her brain inflamed. Turning the garment ever so softly in her hands, like an archeologist inspecting a precious artifact, her wonder amplified when seeing, centered in the triangle, rhinestones in a stylized "A", winking and blinking and sneering.

"UUAAAGGHHH" Claire cried out, her stomach knotted as she covered her mouth. Clenching the thong, she stumbled to her Queen Anne chair next to her dresser, beside the window. Holding the underwear, she sank down, her legs weak, head spinning, eyes filling with tears of anguish and rage. Heaving through sighs and gulps of breath, her heart and soul convulsed for almost an hour as everything else disappeared. This was her worst nightmare; a supreme betrayal painfully discovered. Claire spent the remaining afternoon careening emotionally around and through despair, reviewing her life in marriage, whipping herself with self-loathing and disgust, *"Why didn't I see it? How could I be so stupid?"*

Claire had no hunger, no interest in anything. Reading the digital clock's '6:45', she was stunned; she'd been in her chair almost four hours. Rising slowly, she forced steps down to the kitchen, cajoling herself to eat something, anything. She was alone, the world now uncertain, hostile. She'd forfeited her day to two men; her husband and the naked neighbor.

Forcing down some rotisserie chicken, wild rice and green beans, Claire opened a bottle of wine and poured a glassful. She walked onto the deck and sitting at the table, watched the mountain shadows grow long over the valley. Darkness followed and she lit the three candles sitting at the table's center. She contemplated life going forward with or without Steve. Her cellphone's gyrations snapped her thoughts, chiming and buzzing on the table. The chime told Claire instantly Bryce was calling, confirming his arrival at Tanner's. Claire picked up, "Hey Bryce,"

"Mom, I'm at Tanner's okay."

"Okay,"

"Mom, is anything going on this weekend?"

"What'dya mean?" Claire focused on Bryce.

"Rick, I mean, Mr. Holzworth, got tickets to the Rockies game Saturday night, they're to a box, you know, one of those sky-boxes, they said I can go with. They're going to stay in Denver Saturday night, they said I can go with for the weekend if it's okay with you. Can I go? Please?"

"Oh, honey I don't know, that means you'll be gone all weekend."

"Oh Mom, come on, I'll be back Sunday. It's not like we had anything planned."

Bryce's words stung. Claire stopped to look within her heart, thinking, *"He's right, it's just another weekend to him."*

Claire looked back to the darkness beyond the candle flames, across her backyard, into the night. Alone, she couldn't find any reason to chain Bryce to her distress, "Okay, let me talk to Therese first."

Claire heard Bryce shuffling the phone while exclaiming, "She wants to talk to your mom."

A few moments of waiting before, "Hi Claire, it's Therese."

"So, you're going to a Rockies game?"

"Yeah, Rick's company got a ticket package and gave it to him, so, we're going up to Denver Saturday and we'd love to take Bryce. If it's okay with you."

"Okay, Therese,"

"Yeah,"

"Can you let me know every now and then, how he's doing, and you know, where you're staying and all that please?"

"Sure, I'll text you all the information. I have to get it from Rick, but I'll get it to you by tomorrow afternoon when I pick up the boys from school, okay?"

"That'd be great, thanks Therese."

"Say, it's been a while since we've seen you, how's everything?"

Emotional shields formed, focusing Claire's gaze on a glow coming through the darkness, somewhere beyond her, from the windows of the naked man's house. On auto-pilot, Claire voiced flatly, "Yeah, I'm fine, you know, catalog layout is sucking up my time, but I'm fine."

"We should get together, you know, you, Steve, Rick, for dinner some time."

Claire nearly wretched at the thought of sitting at a dinner table with Steve, but she mustered mild enthusiasm, "Yeah, that's an idea. Can I talk to Bryce now?"

"Sure, okay, take care, I'll get you that information tomorrow, okay?"

"Okay."

Breathless with excitement, Bryce returned. Claire's permission for the weekend was granted and Bryce bubbled with a fourteen-year old's gratitude.

"THANKS MOM!" he gushed, "Thanks a lot."

"Hey, listen to me!" Claire barked over his exhilaration, "You behave yourself young man, you hear me?"

"Yes, yes ma'am, I will. Thank you, Mom, you're the best. I love you, Bye."

The phone went silent. Claire took it from her ear and looked to the now black screen, "At least one Bankord man loves me."

A second glass of wine softened the evening's heartache ever so slightly. Claire thought of various events over the last sixteen years, feeling somehow, she'd been tricked believing those were her true life. Now, in the darkness, she wondered if life played a joke on her, if she'd been cheated, for settling.

Was casting aside aspirations for the rituals of adulthood, real or supposed, ultimately self-defeating? Everything looked different, the sky, stars, the furniture in her house. It felt surreal, no longer comfortable, a station of suspicions, unfriendly, fraudulent. A powerful trap she'd stepped into, clenching, tearing into her flesh, down to her soul.

Returning to her bedroom, she spied the electric pink thong

coiled on the floor. Her wine-polished eyes contemptuously examined the scanty piece. She paused, analyzing it, thinking, 'What is this to me?

She took the sport coat and slacks to the closet, hanging them on the crossbar. Coming out, the thong remained, a beacon of disgust. Claire watched it, lying there, silently mocking her, waiting for another chance to strike.

She looked to her alarm clock: its flame-bright orange '9:50 PM' beamed. No Steve yet, if at all she thought. She went into her closet, undressed and put on her robe. Walking out and tying the sash around her waist, her mind flashed. Bending forward, arms folded across her chest, Claire averred defiantly, "You will not win."

Returning to the closet, she found a group of empty wire hangers on the upper crossbar. Taking one down, she then strode forcefully to the thong, stubbornly lying beneath her eyes, twisted like a small dog under a larger alpha. She bent down and plucked the panty up, sliding it onto the wire hanger, the sparkling 'A' facing her directly. Next, she walked to the bedroom's open double-doors, first pulling the left closed, fixing its latch to the upper threshold. She then pulled the right door almost closed before hanging the pink thong on the door handle; 'A' side out. If Steve came home, he'd find his dry-cleaning waiting. Aloud, Claire pledged, "You will not take from me anymore."

******

25

The cellphone buzzed, jumping from its perch on the nightstand charger next to Claire's bed. Rolling over abruptly, Claire's head muddled and slow, she rubbed her eyes before looking to the ceiling. The ringing and buzzing charged again as she shook herself free of the bedding, sliding her legs over the side, leveraging her torso up. Bright morning light streamed through the east window, glaring, the sun proudly washing the Colorado front range. The ring/buzz erupted again as Claire snatched her bellicose phone. "Hello" she gurgled.

"Claire! You there? My god, I was beginning to wonder."

Folding her free arm across her chest, she held the phone to her ear and looked to her clock, sternly admonishing her with '8:32 AM'. The sunlight searching every surface, her eyes reflexively closed as her free hand rubbed her face, "Hey Renee,"

"Claire, what are you doing?"

Claire looked to the closed doors, still keeping the world away, "What'dya mean?"

"My show, remember, we talked when? Two weeks ago? You were going to have something for me? Some pieces for me?"

Claire's closest friend, Renee Matranga, kept a small gallery featuring local artists in Old Colorado City. Claire met Renee in 2004, shortly after arriving in Colorado Springs. Twelve years older than Claire, Renee occasionally challenged her, asserting her talent wasted in commercial graphic art and design.

"Why do you bother with that crap?" Renee once charged.

"The money's better than most jobs Renee. And I'm here for Steve and Bryce."

"Puaahh, What about you? What are you gonna do for you?"

This morning, Renee came with force, loud, determined and laser-focused on getting Claire's obedience. "So, how've you been? What's going on? Do you have something to show me?"

Standing up from the bed, forgoing her robe, Claire walked over to the doors "I'm working on the Springfield catalog."

"That rag? Why?"

Reaching for the right door handle, Claire replied calmly, "Renee, we've talked about why."

Claire turned the handle and pulled the door open. Twisting free of the door's edge, the pink usurper swung into view, a harpy's laugh wagging to and fro. Claire's stomach tightened as she gasped, "Oh God,"

"What? What's the matter?"

Turning back to the bed, Claire's eyes started filling with tears; Steve's side was still intact. He hadn't come home. Renee waited a three count, then clamored, "Claire! Are you there? Claire!"

Covering her mouth, as her legs buckled, she sank to the floor, her buttocks landing on the carpet, her legs crossed before her. Sobs, muffled by her hand, passed through the cellphone to Renee's ears. "CLAIRE!! Talk to me!" Renee panicked, "Claire, honey, talk to me please!"

"He's not here."

Almost apoplectic, Renee yelled, "WHO'S NOT THERE!?"

Feeling lost, defeated, Claire cried openly. Renee waited a nanosecond, "CLAIRE! WHO'S NOT THERE!?"

Gulping the air, swallowing her despair, Claire lifted the phone to her mouth, "Steve's not here."

"Steve? Where'd he go?" Renee's confusion roiled her sensibilities. "Oh my GOD! What happened to Steve? Is he okay? Claire talk to me! TALK TO ME!"

Claire sobbed and sniffled momentarily before wiping her nose and eyes. Taking a deep breath, she tried composing her mind, realizing she was sitting on her bedroom floor naked. Getting up to put on her robe she answered, "Renee, I'm alright. Steve isn't here. I don't know where he is. Probably with Ashley."

"Ashley? Ashley who? Who's Ashley?"

"His secretary, I guess."

"His secretary? His SECRETARY!? Since when does he have a secretary?"

She forced herself to stand up opposite her dresser mirror. She looked at the nude woman in the reflection, unrecognizable in messed up hair, darkened eyes, flesh sectioned between suntanned or bland. She examined the miserable figure and asked, "Renee, can you come over? I can't talk right now."

"I'm coming over. Don't do anything, I'll be there in fifteen minutes."

******

Renee stormed through the front threshold as Claire, still numb, stood timidly behind the door, wearing only her robe. Eight feet into the house, Renee abruptly turned, her sunglasses searching for her friend hiding in the door's shadow.

"I'm sorry, traffic's a mess everywhere."

"It's okay."

"What's going on? What the hell happened?"

Closing the door, Claire turned and head down, not making eye contact, started walking towards the kitchen. Renee stood and watched her emotionally drained friend pass by, both women silent, both uncertain what to say or think. Approaching the kitchen, Claire softly asked, "Coffee?"

"I'll get it; you go sit down." Renee let her purse plop on the kitchen island as she peeled off her jean jacket. She retrieved a cup from the cabinet, filling it with black coffee. Walking out onto the deck, she blew across the cup's top. Under the table umbrella, sat Claire holding her cup, looking across the yard to the trees and urban expanse to the east-southeast. Renee walked out and looked over Claire's right shoulder, taking in the morning scenery.

"I always love the fragrance of pines and junipers out here," Renee cautiously offered. Taking a sip, Renee walked behind Claire and sat down to Claire's left. The pink thong lay on the table, crumpled yet loud, its rhinestones dulled under the umbrella's shade. The two women sat together in silence, sipping coffee, feeling the occasional breeze float across as the sun crept overhead.

"The world is going on," Claire announced softly, "right out there, everything's the same."

Renee remained quiet, letting her friend set the moment's path and pace.

"I've been tucked away here, thinking I was living while life kept moving on, away from me."

Renee softly asked, "What're you feeling now?"

Claire gazed out, into the air, her arm raising the coffee, lips pursing to sip, her second hand steadying the cup, but her mind, more importantly her heart, was searching somewhere far off. She held the hot solution a moment before swallowing, keeping the cup still, then letting its return arc to the table. She breathed, "I'm not feeling anything, except foolish."

"About what?"

"Years ago, I couldn't leave Wisconsin fast enough. Now what? Go somewhere? Stay?

"Go where?"

"I wanted to live in New York,"

 "Why didn't you?

"Because this dreamy, golden-haired Adonis came to me, said my smile captured his heart, said he was going west, said New York City was a pit."

Renee sipped her coffee, looking to the southern plain, "And where's he from?"

Claire covered her eyebrows with one hand, "Buffalo. There's the pit." Her chagrin pushed her eyelids to the light, her hand coming down to her chin, "Steve said we'd be happy here, like nothing we'd ever seen before."

"And?"

"Colorado is beautiful no doubt, but it's not home." Claire sipped her coffee, slowly, feeling its warmth into her soul, "the geography is incredible, the people, not so much."

"Well, I won't take that personally, but look at what you have," Renee softly rebutted.

"What? This house? I'd sit here many nights and look across the range down to the plains, a million houselights twinkling. Then to the stars above, in deep blue night, shining, shimmering down on me. I'd wonder if anyone else was lonely too?"

"Yes, you have this house," Renee confirmed, "you have a beautiful son, you're healthy, alive, and now you know where your marriage stands. Wake up, quit feeling sorry for yourself. You know I can't stand whiny women."

"You were never afraid, were you."

"Oh, oh ho, ho, ho, honey let me tell you," Renee twisted to Claire, her eyes locked evenly, her smile crocodilian, "Every goddamn day. It's never been easy and I've been scared in ways you can't imagine. But you know what? It's better than sitting at home alone and wondering. Waayy better."

"I'm sorry Renee, I didn't mean to offend," Claire softly offered.

"I get so tired of hearing how every time a woman's miserable, she claims a man made her that way. He's somehow responsible for reducing her to nothing. Somehow, she forgot she has a spine just like his."

Renee's words spit across the table, trapping the lingerie like a net. The friends let the air clear momentarily before Claire spoke, "I convinced myself this was the life I wanted. A wife, a mom, business woman, everything successful. I was foolish, I didn't watch."

Her gaze remained to the southeast, scanning washed out colors and softened edges.

"Did that make you happy?"

Claire's cup went up again, stopping at her lips, "What is happy Renee?"

Before Renee could answer, Claire looked to the distance, "I did what I thought I should do. I was 'Steve's wife' or 'Mrs. Bankord, Bryce's mom', wherever, whenever. Never stopping to figure out if I was happy. I thought sooner or later, happiness would come to me. It didn't."

Renee looked to the deflated thong, now more a wound than a threat. She eyed the piece, asking Claire, "Where'd that come from?"

Claire glanced at the thong, then back to the yard, "The dry cleaners found it for me in Steve's coat pocket."

Renee's chin sagged as anger flashed from her eyes. There was nothing to say, no comforting explanation or justification; here lay prima facie evidence of carelessness, stupidity and disrespect.

Renee calmly asked, "Do you have a lawyer?"

Claire nodded solemnly. They held their mutual silence for a minute, maybe two, before Claire replied, "I'm angry. He wasted my trust, which I gave for so long, never questioning or doubting. I was foolish. It was all too easy."

"You thought you were both in love, the same way, the same time, right?"

Claire nodded again, "I didn't think there was anything else."

Setting aside preparing or applying emotional bandages wherever her friend was bleeding, Renee ventured toward reality, "So, how do you feel about the two of you now?"

Claire resigned, "I'm alone. I'm alone until I can be otherwise."

"Are you comfortable with that?" Renee waited, closely watching Claire.

The women sat together, each reviewing memories and unsatisfying decisions. The air was still, the sun's glare slathering every surface, bright, omnipotent. Renee took a sip and returned her cup to the table. Looking to the far horizon she offered, "Happiness comes and goes. You don't capture it like some wild animal. You find it where you can, knowing you can only hold it in the moment."

Claire looked to the open range, her stare equally broad, "I don't want revenge. I want to move on, where I can be me, just as I am."

"I hate to be the downer here," Renee lifted her palms upward, extending her arms to her sides, her elbows bent, her head swiveling left to right, "But what about all this?"

Holding her empty cup in both palms, Claire smiled, "*I own* all this."

Renee's head twisted slightly right, her left eye squinting, her right eyebrow arched "How?"

"When Steve bought into Gilbert ten years ago, and my business was new, he signed over all his interest in the house to me, in case Gilbert went bankrupt." Claire's knowing smile illuminated her face, "I used my income to pay off the mortgage. I got the deed two months ago."

Renee's mouth dropped open, admiration and approval flowing through her eyes as her hands came back to the table. Letting her amazement momentarily breathe, the thong caught Renee's eye. She reached out, lightly picking up the lace waistband, the 'A' trying to sparkle brightly. Flexing her fingers forward and back, the fabric and rhinestones tilting and flitting, Renee grinned, "I hope this was worth it."

Claire's cellphone chimed in her robe pocket, breaking their shared satisfaction. Pulling the phone out, Claire looked to the screen, "Uugghh, I don't want to talk to you now."

"Who is it?" Renee asked.

"Elyse Leyva," Claire dutifully resigned and pressed the screen, "Hi Elyse."

"Claire? Yeah, hi. Do you know the name of your neighbor?"

"Neighbor, which one?"

"Behind you, he lives in that two story on the cul-de-sac. You know, his trees line up against your fence."

Claire looked to her back fence and the trees beyond. The house was obstructed but the roof could be seen above the tree tops. She pointed her finger toward it and asked, "You mean the light brown house with the dark brown roof?"

"Uh-huh, that's the one. Do you know his name?"

Claire thought a moment, "Uhm, no, never met him."

"Oh? Are you sure?"

Claire's mind flashed, *'I just said I've never met him; how would I know his name?'* She paused, then replied, "No, I don't know his name. I've never met him"

A moment of silence was followed by, "Oh, I was hoping you would know his name."

"Nope, sorry, don't know him."

"Well, have you ever seen him, you know, in his backyard maybe?"

Claire became suspicious at Elyse's interest, "Why?"

"We'll need to talk about it at tonight's committee meeting. You're still coming right?"

Claire put her free hand to her forehead. In the last twenty hours, the meeting had dropped completely from her memory. She didn't want to go, but didn't feel like explaining why; especially to Elyse.

"Well, I'm not sure. I have to see what today brings."

"Claire, it's very important the committee address this issue," Elyse instructed.

"What's the issue? Maybe I can help now." Claire sought to appease and avoid if possible.

"We can't discuss this outside the committee, I told you that yesterday."

Claire's mind snapped, *'My god Elyse, do you have to be so anal about this committee?'* Instead, she held her tongue and waited.

"Well, I guess if you don't know who he is, I'll have to find out from some where's else. But I can count on you for tonight, right?" Elyse was nothing if not singularly self-focused.

"Like I said, let me see how the day goes." Claire committed as far as she could, "If nothing comes up, I'll be there."

"Okay, well, see you tonight then." And Elyse was gone as fast as she arrived.

Claire cancelled the call and laid her phone on the table. Renee took another sip of coffee and while putting her cup down asked, "Who was that?"

"Elyse Leyva, she's the Chairperson, woman, of the neighborhood watch committee."

"What'd she want?" Renee sat back in her chair relaxed and confident normal conversation was possible. Claire shook her head slightly, "I'm not sure. She's calling a committee meeting for tonight about something she won't tell me anything about."

"Why's she calling you?"

"I'm Vice-Chair."

"*Vice-Chair*? What the hell is that?"

"If Elyse can't make a meeting, I sit as the Chairperson, woman, whatever."

"Has that ever happened?" Renee pulled her coffee back to her lips.

"Oh no, Elyse would never miss a meeting." Claire guffed, tossing her head back, running her fingers through her hair, her smile lifting the nights' grief from her eyes. "Neighborhood safety is part of Elyse's *'ministry'* as she calls it."

Renee's eyes widened as she swallowed and she quickly placed the cup back down. Leaning forward in her chair she inhaled deeply, "Wait a minute, wait a minute. Didn't I meet her at your cookout last summer?"

Claire stopped to think as Renee plucked at her lower lip with her index finger, "Let me think, it was, … it was, Labor Day weekend! Remember?" Renee's face lit up and her smile widened, showing her perfect teeth, smooth, white and straight, too perfect.

"You sure?" Claire returned, "I don't think we had anybody over then. You sure it wasn't Fourth of July?"

"You might be right, let me think," Renee looked beyond the backyard and after a moment, her head slowly nodded, "Yeah, I think it was the fourth."

"It was so damn hot, remember? It was what? Ninety-five, ninety-six that day." Claire relaxed back in hear seat, interlocking her fingers, watching Renee search her memory. Renee's nodding sped up with enthusiasm as a well-spring of recollection came to mind. "Yep. I wore those khaki shorts, pleated, with the cuffs, remember? And my white Lauren oxford shirt, the one with the sleeve tabs."

"And those cute guinea dot platforms, I love those. Too bad I can't wear them." Claire smiled.

Renee lifted her right foot, "Honey, nobody but me can wear feet or shoes this big." She shook her head sideways, holding her frown only a moment. Claire thought about the contrast between Renee and Elyse and also shook her head.

Renee McLemore was a six-foot tall, statuesque, auburn-haired vixen who left her small-town Ohio home for Hollywood. Possessing enviably smooth skin, a cleft in her chin under a dazzling smile, her green eyes could flash like camera bulbs, making her irresistible. She got to Las Vegas and needing money, quickly got a job as an exotic dancer.

Only nineteen years old, she was already voluptuous albeit somewhat naïve. Working in a club frequented by patrons of questionable lifestyles and incomes, her height and figure provided Renee certain notoriety. Once, the FBI questioned her knowledge of a money-laundering scheme between the club and some hotels. The club's ownership was never charged and believed Renee's grand jury testimony thwarted the criminal investigation.

A year later Renee left the club and became a hotel review showgirl. Two years later she completed mixologist training and went behind the bar, working five nights a week. She became involved with local wise guy Jimmy "Chops" Matranga. They lived together whenever possible; when Jimmy's wife Marianne didn't complain.

Then Renee became pregnant and things came apart. Marianne went to Jimmy's boss Massimo "Sonny" Lombardo demanding Renee be, *'dealt with.'* Marianne declared she wasn't afraid to cooperate with federal authorities if Sonny didn't act quickly. Sonny listened attentively, smiling and assured her he'd gladly *'take care of everything'.* A week later while shopping at a mall, Marianne disappeared.

A year later, Jimmy married Renee in a civil ceremony and shortly thereafter, whenever home, he routinely found cause to abuse Renee. One night, when eye makeup wouldn't suffice, Renee told some of her hotel 'friends' about Jimmy's hostilities. Sonny Lombardo solved the issue and had an airtight alibi after Jimmy's body was found in a shallow grave outside Flagstaff.

Renee enrolled at UNLV and eventually completed her Bachelor's degree in Art. Renee and her son left Las Vegas, moving to Colorado Springs with Sonny's blessing.

Being well-funded for her move, Renee opened her gallery fifteen years ago. Claire was one of maybe three people Renee trusted with personal confidences.

Occasionally, Renee dated and even less occasionally had romantic relationships. Not because she's afraid, to the contrary; Renee fears no man.

That's her strength and weakness; her confidence makes her alluring to men of integrity; irresistible to those of weaker nature, who think they must control her. Renee lives comfortably without either.

As her foot went back to the deck, Renee's recollection of Claire's party fully illuminated.

"Wasn't she that short, snippy, busybody type. Clipped blond hair, brown roots. A little bottom heavy?"

"Well, I've never thought of her like that but yeah, I suppose so."

"When she heard me say I'd tended bar in Vegas, her face snarled up like I admitted to stealing from my grandmother."

"Really? Why were you talking about that?"

"Somebody asked how you made Long Island Ice Tea? That guy from Steve's company, the owner or president, I think. I told him, from memory. I didn't really think about it." Renee looked out to the landscape, searching for a name.

"Stuart Gilbert?" Claire asked.

"I guess. Anyway, he asked me how I knew and, I didn't think about the people nearby, I said for a while I tended bar in Vegas. It just slipped out."

"What did Elyse say?"

"Nothing, but her face looked like I had the plague or something. She whispered to some snaky looking guy and they stayed away from me all night. Didn't they leave kind of early?" Renee looked back to Claire.

"Yeah, it was Saturday night, they had to go to church the next morning, so I'm sure they left by 9:30." Claire ran her fingers over her forehead and crown, straightening her hair as best she could. "Everything is a 'ministry' with her. Her husband Nick, her children, the watch committee. She's certain the world is out to harm anyone, everyone, and she's here to keep us safe."

"Yeah well, about two weeks later, her husband showed up at my shop, smiling, joking, asking about pieces and prices, slobbering through his cheesy smile. He didn't have a clue, but I knew what he was after." Renee smiled as she peered over the tops of her sunglasses, releasing her all-knowing wink.

"Nick. He's a fireman/paramedic. They've separated twice because he can't keep it in his pants." Claire conceded, "She keeps saying God meant them to be together no matter what Satan tries to do."

"Was that her name? Satan? Weird, I've never met a woman

named Satan," Renee snickered, "I wonder if God said it was okay because it was only a woman named Satan?"

Claire chuckled at Renee's snark, seasoned with jaundiced frustration. Claire asked the open blue sky, "How long does it take a man to stop thinking with his dick and use his brain instead?"

Hearing that, Renee felt her presence to protect Claire no longer necessary. Fixing her sunglasses snugly against the bridge of her nose, she stood up, "Listen kiddo, you sound like you're okay for now. I need to get back, but if you need anything or want somebody around or anything, you call me, hear?"

Bending over toward Claire, Renee put her arms over Claire's shoulders, "I mean it, promise you'll call me."

"I will, I promise." Claire reached up into Renee's embrace "Thanks for coming. I'll be okay, really."

"Have any ideas on what you're going to do?" Renee asked, standing up to full height.

"Oh, I have plenty. Right now, I'm just going to wait and see what he does."

"That's my girl" Renee smiled and while walking into the house called back "Love you, call me!"

"Love you too!" Claire called back.

Broken Windows, Renovated Souls

******

It was almost 1:30 in the afternoon when Claire shopped for groceries. She showered, dressed and made a chicken-salad sandwich for lunch. Some potato chips and pickle spear completed the meal. Sitting at her kitchen island, Claire ate her sandwich with one hand while making a list with the other. Upon finishing the chips, Claire tore the sheet off the pad and gathered her recycled grocery bags. Thirty minutes later she was pushing a cart down the aisles, looking for the items written down and any others that caught her eye.

Turning down a refrigerated aisle, she began searching for frozen beef patties or chicken tenders. Ahead to her left, one door was opened, a cart to its right and what looked like someone searching inside. The glass clouded with condensation, Claire wasn't sure if it was a man or woman. She stopped eight feet behind the open door and peered through the cold glass portal to her left, eyeing multiple brightly colored packages of tater-tots of various names and configurations, but potatoes for oven roasting just the same. Stepping ahead of the cart, Claire walked to the glass doors showing pre-assembled meals. She could hear the person behind the clouded door talking; it was a man.

Claire spied the burger patties she wanted in the section immediately left of the open door. She hoped to just reach in, get one bag and be gone. Sliding up to the spot, she reached for the handle and quietly, evenly, pulled it open. The door swung toward her as she stepped around it and bent down to grab the plastic package.

"Just pick one for god's sake," the voice commanded.

Startled by the edict, Claire froze, looking to the opaque door, the form behind seeming to burrow, shake and fuss. Again, the voice came out, "All these years, and never once thought about what she was cooking. Why?"

Claire pretended to not hear the monologue, but her proximity made it so easy. The man stood up from the cavern's entry, a package in his hand. He looked to the information panel, reading closely, his lips moving with the words. His head bobbed up and through the frost smoked door he looked to Claire. Without guile or mendacity, he boldly asked, "You ever had these? Are they any good?"

Claire held her patties, her face open, eyes unblinking, "I'm sorry, what'd you say?"

Taking a step back, letting the door close, the man lifted the package up a little higher, shifting it towards her. "These 'plant-based burgers'; you ever had them? They any good?"

Claire listened to his tone, he wasn't aggravated; he was doubtful, he didn't know. Slightly taller than Claire, probably in his mid-fifties, tanned and still in good shape. Wearing shorts, deck shoes and a large-print Hawaiian type shirt, his salt and pepper hair was neatly combed, still full and well cared for. She looked to the bag, back to his face and back to the bag, only to ask, "Well, what's it say on the back?"

"It sounds like their healthy, but I don't know, who can you believe anymore, you know?"

Even at the grocery store, life was challenging Claire's understanding and awareness. She considered his question and while thinking, his smile began to relax her and dispel her uncertainty. She laughed lightly, "That's a good question, who you can believe anymore?"

He turned the package in his hands so Claire could review the dietary information panel with him. For a few moments they both scrutinized the numbers, chemicals and nutrients stated on the label before looking to each other.Eye to eye, they looked, then shrugged as Claire offered, "There's nothing that looks bad, so I don't know. Guess you'll have to try them."

His eyes softened and his smile broadened, "You're her, the

neighbor behind me. Up there on the hilltop." Now the package dropped as he turned to face Claire completely, his smile still broad, his eyes still engaging, sunglasses tracks sliding back towards his ears. Claire stood quiet, not sure what to say but realizing the depth of his tan; it was him, the naked lawn-mowing neighbor.

"I live in the two-story, just behind your fence, I have the Blue Spruce's and Aspens?"

"Oh, is that your house?" Claire feigned ignorance. Feeling slightly awkward, she extended her right hand to shake, "Hi, I'm Claire Bankord, nice to meet you."

His smile stayed fixed as his hand took her hand, covering it fully, gently clenching but not crushing, "I'm Leonard. Leonard Stines. Nice to meet you Claire Bank…Bankord? Is that correct?"

As their hands rose and dropped three times, Claire smiled and replied, "Yes. Yes, it is."

Breaking the handshake, Leonard then stated, "You had the big party last Fourth of July."

"Oh, it wasn't that big."

"Yeah, it was. Kept me up till' almost one in the morning."

"Oh, I'm sorry, I didn't know."

"You know how you eliminate any complaints don't you?"

Her face returning to that of a school girl, closed mouth, wide eyes, waiting, she shook her head slightly left to right, "No, how?"

"Invite your neighbors. Give em' at least a chance to say no."

"I'm always worried someone will call the police." Claire stammered, looking to the floor.

"Yeah, well, years ago I was the police. Believe me, if you tell your neighbors in advance, my experience, they rarely complain." Leonard tossed the bag of plant-based burger patties into his cart.

"Are you still a policeman?"

"Detective," He nodded, "I retired a detective. Chicago." His smile beamed, "Thirty-two years on the job."

"Oh, so what do you do now?"

"Whatever I want. That's what retirement's all about. How about you, what do you do?" Leonard put his hands into his pockets, relaxed, shoulders rounded, happy to be conversing.

"I'm a graphic artist, I do catalogs and advertisements and marketing displays. I have a studio in my house."

"Niiccee," Leonard nodded, "How about your husband, what's he do?"

Asking about Steve caught Claire off-guard. She'd wanted to avoid thinking about him since Renee left. Now, trying to appear normal, Claire struggled to think about how to speak of Steve, "He's, he's, a, vice-president, for a construction company."

"Well, good for him."

'Come on Leonard,' Claire thought, *'He's cheating on me.'* Claire asked, "And your wife, what's her name?"

Leonard's eyes softened as his smile deflated, "Louise, her name was Louise."

"Was?"

"She died two years ago. Cancer."

Aghast at her insensitivity, Claire quickly raised her hand to her mouth, "Oh, I'm so sorry, please forgive me!"

"No, it's okay, you didn't know. It's okay, really." Leonard took one hand from his pocket and gently extended his arm toward Claire, palm facing her. His smile stayed, his eyes still charming in their sparkle, but his persona now softer to Claire, molded to his demeanor, casual, unconcerned. He paused for a moment, then stated calmly, "It was sudden, she'd been sick, but we didn't think it was anything serious. By the time we got the diagnosis, she had three-to-six months. She went in two. Fortunately, with the pain meds, she didn't suffer all that much."

"I'm so sorry. I shouldn't have said anything." Claire felt mortified until the image of him popped into her mind. Perplexed, Claire wanted to hear more as Elyse's questions now also echoed, juxtaposed against mental imagery of Leonard crossing his backyard, pushing his lawnmower, nude.

"So, how are you now?" Claire asked, the question sounding foreign, like it came from some other part of her.

His hand went back into his pocket and with a shrug, he looked down to his right, "Today, I'm okay, I guess. I mean, some days I struggle but, you know." He looked back to her, his face now normal, not twisted or clouded by grief, simply looking to Claire. Then, a most interesting statement came from Leonard, "Some days, I'm scared. Look at me, fifty-six years old, married for thirty years and some days, I can't find my feet."

His stare drifted across the floor between them, then he looked to her, "I realized about four or five months ago, being alone wasn't a punishment. I'm where I am now because of choices I, and Louise, made. Now, life's different and I've got to live."

Intrigued, Claire tilted her head, "How does that work?"

"Once I accepted Louise was no longer here, I decided to live each day like I wanted, like I was about to find the most beautiful moment, doing whatever, whenever, wherever."

Claire listened intently, wondering what her life might be if she lived as she wanted, whenever, wherever? What would be important enough to continue? She looked to the package in his cart, "Did she buy you these?"

Leonard looked back, then quickly jerked his head and smiled, "No!" he laughed, "I'm trying something new, part of my new life."

He smiled, looking again into the space between them, bemused, surprised by his admission.

"How do you know you're doing it right?" Claire asked, her heart waiting.

Leonard smirked, raising his right hand to his lips, pursing them between index finger and thumb. He thought carefully and then tilted his head slightly forward, in a stage whisper he replied, "I don't worry about what anyone else thinks, or says, or does. The fact that I wake up each morning is satisfaction enough. I keep to myself, be respectful of others and smile whenever possible. I decide each day, it's my life; nobody else's business. And you know what?"

Transfixed, Claire leaned forward, "What?"

"I sleep like a baby every night." Leonard's smile returned to full volume as his hand came forward, "Well, it's been a pleasure meeting you Claire Bank, …"

"Bankord," Claire nodded, taking his hand to shake again.

"Bankord, yes, I need to go now, it was nice meeting you."

The three shakes completed, Leonard turned to his cart, placed his hands on the crossbar and looking back smiled, "Bye now."

Claire watched Leonard walk away, noticing a smooth, steady gait as he turned right at the end of the aisle. The rest of her time shopping, Claire weighed every word of Leonard's last statements,

'It's my life; nobody else's business,' echoing against the occasional, *'I sleep like a baby'.* She wondered as she looked for ice cream, *'what is my life?'*

She asked herself, 'do I really care what other people think?' Passing the magazines, breath mints, candy bars and AA battery packs at the checkout station, Claire carefully considered this turning point, ruminating, *'In four years Bryce will go to college. Even if Steve and I somehow remained together, how could I ever trust him?'*

As her basket was unloaded, item after item scanned, Claire silently examined her feelings, Steve's infidelity, turning forty-two years old. Yes, she was older, no escaping that but, beyond hope or happiness? Claire refused that question. As she walked with her cart full of bags, she heard Renee's voice, *'Happiness comes and goes; you hold it in the moment.'* Stopping at her car door, she declared to the mountains, "My happiness will be my happiness."

******

Seven people came to the one-story Canyon View Park Fieldhouse next to the community park, tennis courts and playground. Down a hall from the main room just beyond the lobby, the Canyon View Neighborhood Community Watch Group filed into a modest sized conference room. The room kept a ten-foot table with eight chairs surrounding it.

Heated and cooled by the locked thermostat, the room air was brisk. Immediately right of the doorway stood a small table, on the left wall two bookcases, the imitation mahogany laminate type, waited. On the north wall opposite the bookcases, two windows allowed ambient light to compliment the ceiling lights.

Claire parked her car and reluctantly walked to the fieldhouse doorway. The interior lighting was brighter than evening dusk and through the far-right window she saw Elyse sitting at one end of the conference table. She pulled the door open and paused to question herself, *'do I really want to do this?'*

Feeling no response, she entered, robotically turned down the hall, walking to the meeting without interest or energy, repeating another life thing out of habit. The conference room light triggered her smile as she entered and walked to an open chair at the table's end, opposite Elyse. She smiled with hollow cheer, "Hi everybody,".

"Good," Elyse stated, "Everyone's here. Let's get started. I'd like to call this meeting to order, are there any objections?"

Six heads nodded in agreement, bobbing in their own rhythms. An older gentleman, 'Robert' a white-haired retiree, having thick sausage-like fingers, raised one hand while nodding.

A thin brown-haired lady, 'June' leaned her cheek against her left-hand knuckles as her right hand recorded the meeting's time and attendees on a legal pad.

Looking at her position, the sloped shoulders, torso tilted forward, you could easily imagine the cigarette that once hung from the right corner of her mouth, its smoke drifting upward. Her hands were so painfully thin, you could see bones, tendons, veins and sinew just beneath her age-spotted skin.

Claire brought her own steno pad because she liked keeping notes to pass the time. Claire rarely initiated any topic or question, preferring to watch, listen, and vote when asked. Others may have thought her studious and attentive, but never asked what she recorded or thought.

Grasping the members' acquiescence, Elyse proceeded. Opening her red vinyl portfolio, she flipped forward two legal pad sheets. Taking out her purple-ink ball point pen, she clicked it open and looked around the table, her face solemn, eyes blinking twice before returning to the pad. "A very alarming situation has come to my attention."

"I was informed that we may have a sexual predator in our neighborhood." Again, with eyes slightly wider, she looked to each person.

Claire did not make eye contact, writing 'sex pred' on her pad. A collective gasp went up, members' heads turned left and right, as if the predator was amongst them. Looking stunned, Robert interlaced his fingers and placed them on the table as he leaned forward and asked, "Who is it?"

Everyone but Claire watched Elyse, who sat waiting, tapping her pen against her legal pad. Finally, Claire looked up and believing she held everyone's full attention, Elyse pronounced in a grave, serious voice, "His name is Leonard Stines."

Another, lesser gasp went up before a member, a woman who's name Claire could never remember asked, "Who's Leonard Stines?"

Claire sat still, watching the others twist in their seats, unsettled by Elyse's allegation. Elyse also watched, tapping her pen, waiting to further control the meeting. She started nodding her head, "I know, I know, I was shocked when I heard it."

"Where does this Leonard live?" Robert asked.

"He's on the Peregrine Close cul-de-sac and I, uhm," Elyse pulled one of the sheets back to review, "I think he moved here about five years ago."

June wrote smoothly, her eyes never leaving the page before her. Robert kept his hands on the table, fingers still laced, tips extended. Claire sat still and thought back to her meeting Leonard in the grocery store. Silently, she mentally wrestled with Elyse's statement; she couldn't reconcile her impression of a sexual predator with the man she met. Did she misread him? Clearing her throat, Claire asked, "A sexual predator. How do you know that?"

The murmuring assembly paused, looking to Claire and then, considering the question, to Elyse. Seeing everyone's face, Elyse swallowed and replied, "A concerned neighbor came to me."

"And said he was a sexual predator?" Claire asked, her face twisting slightly at her left cheek, "Who's this concerned neighbor?"

"I can't say, I promised confidentiality," Elyse fudged.

"Why not?" Robert asked, "That's a pretty serious charge."

Again, the older woman asked, "Who's Leonard Stines"

June's eyes shifted right, then left, then back to the pad, her writing never stopping. Tension crept up from the floor as Elyse sat back in her chair, quickly glancing at various members. Sensing a need to assert control, she resumed, "A neighborhood resident came to me. She believed this man is a threat, to children."

Claire's grew suspicious of Elyse's claim, "Who said he's a sexual predator? The police? Does he have a record?"

"I don't know, I only got his name today." Elyse tried regaining the lead. "But we've got to be careful, we could get sued."

"Sued?" Robert reacted, "Why would we get sued?"

"Look," Elyse countered, "people said that he walks around his yard naked, in broad daylight, anyone can see."

A swirling frustration rekindled in Claire, "Elyse, do you know if he's been convicted or anything?"

Elyse looked to Claire, eyes wide, her cheeks reddening, her pen-holding hand trembling. Locking her eyes onto Claire's, Elyse charged, "We are responsible for neighborhood safety."

Likewise, Claire focused on Elyse as the others melted from view, "Elyse, who reported this to you? Who said he was a sexual predator?"

"He was walking around his backyard, mowing his lawn, then laid on his lawn-chair, massaging his" her face contorting as her head shook, "you know, himself."

Claire detected discomfort shaking Elyse's righteousness. With measured tone, Claire asserted, "*You* saw him, didn't you Elyse."

Elyse froze, her glare examining within. The others froze too, eyes wide, some mouths surprised open. Elyse squirmed in her chair, straightening her body upward, folding her hands together, pen standing up between her palms.

"I saw him walking around his backyard, naked. Then he went

up to his deck, sat on his lounge chair. He rubbed lotion all over his body." Her chin lowered as her eyes rose to her eyebrows, "*ALL OVER HIS BODY*, his, you know."

Annoyed, Claire demanded an explanation. "How could you see him from your backyard?"

"I wasn't in my backyard. I was on the bike path."

Claire gasped, astounded, "The bike path? You saw him from the bike path? The bike path that goes through the lowest part of our neighborhood. When?"

"Yes." Elyse nodded, chin thrust forward in righteous defiance, "I was walking on the path yesterday morning and I saw him through his fence."

"And from that you figured he was naked, and massaging himself and a sexual predator?" Indignant, Claire rhythmically shook her head from side to side, like a school teacher chastising a student.

"I saw him through a knot-hole! He mowed his lawn, then went up to his deck!" Elyse snapped.

New murmurings in unclear language rolled over the table, a bath of disappointment and distrust. Robert sat back, folding his arms across his chest, looking down to his left. June stopped her motion, looking at Elyse with disbelief. Thinking she could salvage her crusade, Elyse retorted, "He took a bottle of lotion and started rubbing himself! Right there on his deck! In broad daylight!"

Laughter, softly bubbled up, relieving the moment's intensity. Claire sat motionless, amazed by Elyse's audacity.

"Elyse, maybe he was naked, okay?"

"No maybe! He was NAKED!"

"Okay, he was naked. But in his own backyard. Did you ever think he could've been putting on sunscreen?"

Now twittering laughter and chagrined embarrassment floated as some smiled, laughing, scratching their heads, acknowledging private property rights, uncomfortable or otherwise. Desperate to recapture her momentum, Elyse turned on Claire, "He lives behind you, have you ever seen him, naked?"

Elyse's question pivoted the room's focus like a judo move onto Claire. The others now suddenly wondered what Claire may have seen. Trying to diffuse their scrutiny, she put her hands on the table, "What I've seen isn't the question. The question is,"

"Have you ever seen him naked Claire? It's a simple question." Elyse's tongue settled into her left cheek as she sat back, confident she'd defeated Claire's challenge. Claire calmly eyed Elyse replying, "It's his property. What he does by himself is no concern of ours."

"Claire, have you ever seen him naked in his backyard?" Elyse pressed.

Claire paused, tried to maintain a brave face, "Do you have a police report, is he on a register, has someone filed a complaint against him?"

Elyse was quaking, her eyes bulging above red cheeks, she leaned forward, pen in hand, "HAVE YOU SEEN HIM NAKED? YES, OR NO?"

"NO, I HAVE NOT!" Claire shot back, "How dare you!"

The atmosphere suddenly electric, everyone took long, deep breaths. In awkward silence each member wondered what would happen next; little gestures, hand movements, shifting in seats, fidgeting without sound. Claire watched Elyse, who looked to every other member before returning her gaze to Claire. Seeing Elyse stalled, uncertain, Claire spoke firmly, without care.

"You invaded his privacy. You went to his fence and looked through a knot-hole." Claire waited momentarily, then challenged, "Were you on one of your 'prayer walks' Elyse? The walk's you go on when you're struggling at home?"

Elyse sat frozen, her face bright red.

"*You* decided he was a sex predator because he wasn't wearing clothes in his own backyard. *You* called us together and *you* want us to do something about nothing. *You* think you can say whatever and people will do whatever because *you* say so. *You* beat people with your religion so *you* can feel good about yourself." Claire's fury buttressed her disgust with this suburban zealot, someone without charm or personality, coercing or convicting everyone in the name of Jesus.

"I am a woman of God, my ministry here on earth, is to protect us from the works of the evil-one." Elyse raised her chin, looking into the air, "This is a fallen world needing us true believers to share the glory of Christ."

"Oh, Elyse please, spare me." Claire's head turned left and she looked away. Every time Elyse was stymied, her religion and ministry came forward, a panacea for her feelings of inadequacy.Claire witnessed it at committee meetings, cookouts, parent-teacher nights, even in super-market checkout lines.

Now, caught lying, spreading dangerous allegations that could ruin someone's life, Elyse raised her religion to justify her reckless conduct.

"Just because he's not wearing clothes, in his own backyard Elyse, doesn't mean he's a predator or something evil. Remember, Adam started out naked too." Claire admonished.

"Oh? What's he going to do naked? Just lay around? Pppssshhh!" Elyse folded her arms across her chest. She sat back momentarily, then charged again, "I'll tell what he's going to do; he's going to find someone, something to screw!"

"Not every man is like Nick or Steve, Elyse."

Claire closed her eyes, astounded her thoughts became clear, audible, echoing through the small room, cutting to the bone. Now the air took on density as five sets of eyes between Elyse and Claire all expanded, some mouths forming, 'oh,' but no sounds coming forth.

Elyse clenched her hands, her fingertips turning white, tears forming in her ducts. She'd been struck by lightning, the truth of her life, piercing her deeply. There it was, before those she once commanded, now reducing her to a mere mortal.

Claire wanted to apologize but couldn't form the words, her mind still churning with contempt. She watched Elyse quietly close her folder, click her pen and reach down to the floor for her purse. Taking a deep breath, Elyse slowly rose; standing at the table's end, she softly announced, "I'm leaving. If anyone wants to discuss this further, you can call me."

She stepped to her right and with head up, eyes forward, walked out of the room. The other six members mute, June's writing stopped a moment later. Everyone looked to one another and then began pushing their seats away from the table. Without any declaration or vote, Robert said, "Well, I guess the meeting's over."

As the members slowly, quietly left, walking back to their lives, Claire sat, re-hearing herself challenging Elyse, re-visualizing member's heads like a tennis audience, slapping left and right. Elyse's fervor and indignation surprised Claire, but not as much as the fury churning within. She wondered how Elyse could make such claims about Leonard? To Claire's knowledge, she'd never met or interacted with Leonard. Hell, she didn't even know his name until today.

Claire's mind returned to the chance meeting in the grocery store aisle, his smile, his casual demeanor. Was that a ruse? A guise meant to distract her from distrust or suspicion? No, Claire was sure of her instincts. Leonard may be suffering, but he didn't seem interested in inflicting suffering. Claire left his conversation believing he, much like she, was facing a difficult time. But Elyse's attitude, her furious cynicism about Leonard's intentions, clothed or otherwise, was that Elyse's disappointment in her marriage? In herself?

Pushing the chair back, Claire stood up, took her pad and pen, then pulled her purse up onto her left shoulder. Placing the chair back to the table's edge, she quietly turned off the light and left the room. Walking through the center front doors, she looked to the dark blue evening sky, striped from the west with the last purple-red-orange rays of the sun. The air was crisp under a breeze that rolled down from the mountains and through the neighborhood streets. There were things to consider tonight, some easy, some not so easy. As she approached her car, Claire believed these meditations would require a sweatshirt, no bra, some wine and a lit candle on the deck at home. And ice cream, contemplations of this caliber demanded the wine be with ice cream.

Driving home from the grocery store, Claire wondered how the discord between Elyse and Nick came to be. Was he always a bad boy and she thought her faith would correct him? Did he grow tired of her? Deciding instead that infidelity was less problematic than trying to reinvigorate their marriage? Maybe he was one of those men who had a compulsive sex addiction?

Steve was always smooth, smiling, smart. Claire suspected a 'dirty side' to his choirboy persona; she never thought it would hurt her. Occasionally, lusty, insecure women would comment in her presence about his hair, his dimple, his height, but Claire only thought them desperate. Now, Claire wondered, would she be desperate?

Whatever the explanation, the symptoms seemed universal, a woman wakes up each day, diligently tries making her best life only to be diminished, abandoned or betrayed by the man she wanted to be hers and hers alone, leaving her scrambling to make sense of life, her security, herself. As the garage door slowly rose before her, the back bumper, taillights and rear of Steve's SUV emerged, a hulking gray-black mass returning her problems between them.

"Oh God," Claire breathed softly to her windshield. She turned her car off and sat in the vehicle's reflected light, glowing up around her. Looking to the empty space ahead, she asked, "Why is this happening, like this, now,to me?"

She spied the door into the kitchen, the passage to her daily existence, now foreboding, dark. She prepared for the unknown, thinking she must remain calm, she'd done nothing wrong, had nothing to fear. But she was afraid, very uncertain and her stomach tightened as she lifted the door handle, a voice from somewhere between her brain and her diaphragm confronted her, *"Claire, when will you live? When will it be time for your world? The one you've always wanted to see?"*

She clenched the wine bottle neck under the paper bag and felt the ice cream container resist her lift. Once out of the car, she took a deep breath, secured her purse on her shoulder and shifted the wine and ice cream to her left hand. With cautious determination, she walked to the door, walking softly, waiting to hear or see something.

Except for the stove light, her house was dark, quiet. Across the kitchen island and into the family room, soft illumination reached the fireplace. Waiting for her eyes to adjust, Claire looked to the sliding doors that led to the deck. The blackness outside returned reflections at various angles. A muffled sound from the second floor gave Claire momentary relief; Steve was in the bedroom.

Retrieving a bowl and soup spoon, Claire opened the ice cream, digging out three sizeable lumps. With her ice cream waiting, she pulled the wine-opener out of the drawer. Quickly, she turned the corkscrew, set the lever-handle and with a sudden lift, almost pulled the cork out. Taking the handle firmly in hand, a second quick motion produced a cartoon-like "poop." Claire retrieved a tall stemmed, globe-shaped glass from the upper cabinet. With the long pour ended and cork returned to the bottle, she slipped the wine bottle under her right arm, lifted the bowl and glass and proceeded to the deck. The candles were lit, the wine was sipped and she relaxed.

"Oh, there you are" Steve said from behind the family room screen door.

Claire did not respond, quietly taking another spoonful of ice cream, waiting.

"I guess we should talk," he slid the screen door aside and walked out to the table. Approaching the chair to Claire's left, he pulled it out, turning it slightly towards the backyard, not facing Claire directly, instead looking out into the night. Claire watched him, remaining silent, holding her outrage on a mental leash. Steve sat down, his face serious, folding his hands in his lap, a grimace came when he twisted his body toward her, "I'm sure you're upset with me," he began, "but it's not what you think."

Letting a spoonful of ice cream melt on her palate, Claire wondered to herself, *Upset? Is that what you think Steve? Upset?*

"Three weeks ago, when I had that meeting at the Claremont Hotel, with the shopping mall people, remember?" Steve looked to the blackness again, it was easier that way. "That," he paused, now clearly discomforted, uneasy, *"thing* you found,"

"THING" her mind jumped, *"you call it a 'thing' like I'm ignorant?"* Her anger, while building, was tempered by her curiosity at Steve's awkward attempt to rationalize.

"Ashley was at the meeting, and, she got up to go to the bathroom, and well, when she picked up her purse, it fell out, on the table. I grabbed it without knowing what it was and put it in my pocket, to save both of us from embarrassment." Now he turned slightly, making the side-glance less difficult, "I know it looks bad, but honestly, it was nothing."

Claire swallowed her last portion of ice cream and took a sip of wine, flavors colliding as she measured her thoughts, her breathing, her response. She was disappointed in realizing Steve truly believed he could manage her feelings with such a horrible explanation. She looked up to see Steve watching, waiting for a sign, acceptance that life could go on. Claire thought, *"I'll be damned if anything will be like before."*

Before Claire could voice a syllable, Steve resumed, "Anyways I'm letting Ashley go, she's not that bright."

"Oh, oh well, that makes all the difference Steve. You use her until there's a problem, or are you now using me?" Claire's disappointment morphed into growing disgust, amazed at Steve's banal pose, she took another sip of wine. Turning his chair back toward the table, Steve leaned forward, "You understand, don't you? It's a simple misunderstanding."

"Steve stop."

"Claire, I know you're upset."

"Stop talking Steve. You don't know anything." Claire's words were smooth, her tone moderate, her head nodding slightly as she looked to the night beyond the candles.

"Claire, what do you want me to say? I love you. I should've returned it to Ashley that night."

"Which night Steve? The night of the meeting or some other night? Don't bother, it's time we face ourselves."

"What are you talking about?" His face open.

"I'm not the Claire you think Steve."

"What?"

"I don't trust you."

"Wait a minute Claire, I told you, this was an innocent mistake." His voice now began a singing, whiny float. "I picked it up to avoid embarrassment, for the company, myself, Ashley too I guess."

"Steve, you could have done it for the Pope, I don't care. I can't trust you. I don't believe you really care about me."

"How can you say that? Look at all I've done for you, everything we've done over the years." A tinge of frustration now surfaced just under his supplication.

"Steve, I've been thinking about our wedding day, remember how Dad and I were a little late, coming down the aisle?"

Steve shrugged, trying to appear knowledgeable but unable to recall, "Yeah, kind of,"

"Dad stopped me in the lobby, before we turned into the church, he said, 'Watch this guy Claire.' I thought he was just being, you know, Dad."

"All fathers distrust their son-in-laws."

"No, no dad was right." Claire took a larger sip of wine, letting it smoothly roll down her tongue and throat, "I was wrong. I thought he was unfairly suspicious. I thought I knew better and so I didn't watch, I just went along because it was easier. I settled with the myths of married life, repeated by people who didn't know any better."

"What's wrong with our marriage?"

"Each day, it's okay, so long as I keep you and Bryce moving forward." She looked into Steve's eyes squarely, not blinking or flinching.

"So now Bryce is a problem?"

"Don't try to change the subject Steve," Claire's maternal instinct began stoking her rage, "Bryce is not a problem Steve." She rested the wine glass in her hand, the stem between the middle and ring fingers. Feeling momentum, Claire continued, "I've been willing to look away, accept the status quo because it was easier. I bet you thought I didn't care."

"Claire, I never thought that."

"Really Steve? When was the last time we had sex, spur of a moment, when Bryce was out of the house?"

Steve's face froze, blank, unable to recall any intimacy. He stared at the candles briefly before looking to her, "Thanksgiving, remember, after he went to Tanner's house to play video games."

"Jackie and Doug were here, so were your parents. No, it was last Valentine's Day, Bryce went to Boulder on a field trip. Over a year ago Steve," her head turned as she looked back to the night, softly announcing, "and it wasn't that good."

"No. You're wrong." Steve shook his head, a frown now pulling his face down.

"Steve, a woman doesn't confuse intimacy; something she keeps in her heart."

The still, cool air hung between them, occasionally brushing the candles flames to one side, the night wrapping around them. The silence confirmed each person's realization of how little they thought about each other. Watching the flickering candlelight, each pondered the next statement, next step, next decision. Finally, Steve asked, "What are you going to do? What do you want Claire?"

Leaning back in her chair, Claire inhaled deeply, holding her breath as her eyes lifted to the umbrella ribs spread above her. Smoothly, she announced, "I want to be free Steve, free in my life. I want to be the way I want to be. Not doing, just being, unafraid, happy."

"Where you gonna' do that?"

"Right here Steve." She smiled to the center pole, it's brass fittings reflecting her growing confidence.

A sneer, ever so slight, began building at Steve's chin, working its way up to his lips, his eyes squinting, his head tilting back "What'd you mean?"

"Steve, I own the house. You signed it over to me when you bought into Gilbert, remember?"

"It's marital property, I'll get half."

"And I can get half your ownership in Gilbert." Again, Claire's eyes were fixed on his, unblinking, unafraid.

Steve sat, his index finger rubbing small circles on the inside of his thumb, his mind churning under Claire's cool savvy. He didn't recognize the woman sitting before him. After some quiet moments, he shifted the chair back, "So, that's how you want this? Just like that, one mistake and it's over?"

"Yes, Steve, it has to be."

His anger moved from insulted to desperate, "What am I supposed to do?"

"I've thought about that too. I'll let you stay in the guest bedroom for two weeks, that's all." She raised her glass to her lips while quickly glancing. The glass returned to the table and she continued, "Of course, we're going to have to explain this to Bryce, soon."

"How can you do this to me?" Steve pleaded, his face wrinkling. He waited, looking to her longingly, suddenly vulnerable, not the cocksure golden boy she met in college. Sitting back in the chair, with spread fingers he brought their tips together, thumb-tips to his lips, "Where'd we go Claire? What happened to us?"

Setting her hands on the wine glass base, she leaned forward, watching her hands, the glass stem, "I will not be a woman who accepts the indifferences or insults of others, who acted without giving me a thought. Me, as a person, my life, deserves better. If I have to be single to be satisfied, I'm willing to do just that. I refuse to let anyone's weakness steal my happiness."

They sat in silence, each focused inward. There were no responses following Claire's declaration, no arguments, no pleas, just candle flames occasionally shifting in the breeze. Five minutes later Steve left.

Claire brooded into the darkness, the breeze clearing her mind, the wine soft, comforting, wrapping new assurance around each thought of anticipation, of life as a new person, single, left to her own choices. What could such a life hold for her?

Claire looked to the sky, stars twinkling down, gazing directly from the heavens to her. The universe felt welcoming, a host long awaiting a weary traveler, late in the night, a series of single lanterns guiding the sojourner home. She asked the heavens aloud, "What would my life be like, just myself, from here?"

The breeze floated softly across her cheeks, lightly crisping their edges. She waited, listening, wanting to hear not just any answer, no, it must be the right answer.

"What should my life be from now on?" she asked the heavens, hoping the subtle change would arouse universal interest, compelling a response.

The breeze flickered the candle flames but avoided Claire's skin. Another sip of wine and Claire watched the brightened flames slowly return to traditional shape, their usual intensity. Wondering if the surrounding night held answers but no interest, she looked to the southern sky, black, hovering over the valley, its stars fading to the horizon.

A light gust, opposite the last flow, coming from the northeast, pushed into Claire's forehead, touching her face and throat as a voice asked, "What *could* your life be, going on from here?"

******

Claire awoke Saturday to a bold sky layered with orange-yellow-pink-blue strands of sunlight streaming into her bedroom. Another clear, bright, splendid Colorado morning. The coffee-maker's gurgling stirred the quiet house as Claire took her cup out to the deck, returning to last night's seat thinking only of today.

Breakfast was light and quick. Cleaning up for one was effortless, choosing to wash the dishes by hand, letting them dry on the counter. She reviewed the mail on the kitchen island, mostly addressed to Steve, thinking, *'He'll have to change his address.'*

She went to her studio, this catalog had to be finished and despite loathing the process, Claire embraced the necessity of client pleasing, keeping them satisfied, retaining their business.

Working the entire morning, she stopped when her digital clock read, '01:40'. Looking out the windows, she relished the bright blue midday sky. She closed her small tool box that held drawing pencils, erasers, markers and some bits of cloth. Wearing only her underwear and tee-shirt, Claire decided to dress.

She walked to her bedroom where, after a moment's doubt, she pulled out running shorts and a tank top. Foregoing the tee-shirt, she changed and went downstairs, out on the deck, the sun beaming down.

Claire realized the grass was surprisingly deep in some spots, unruly, rampant, darker green eruptions clumped here and there. Scanning her entire property, she was engulfed by quiet, peaceful air. Her yard, the fence, tall and brown contrasting the emerald grasses waving under the slight breeze, energized Claire. She descended the deck stairs to the patio announcing, "The yard needs mowing."

Her steps bounced across the concrete, propelling her jauntily to the storage shed between the house and south fence. Lifting the latch, she pulled the two doors open, letting sunlight and fresh air enter before her. She pushed the lawnmower, rolling it into full sunlight, the grass catcher following. Remembering her father's instructions, she unscrewed the gas cap and squinted into the empty tank.

Popping up, she spied the gas can inside the shed. She lifted the can, shook it hard and heard fuel sloshing within, then returned to the waiting mower. This wasn't difficult, not the dredge Bryce frequently lamented or masculine challenge Steve insisted. It was a chore, but also an escape, something less complicated, functional exercise, something to lose yourself in to escape life and time.

Returning to the mower, Claire recalled rote learning from decades ago. She held the control bar with her left hand, her arm straight, muscles flexed. She took the starter handle in her right hand and taking a deep breath, yanked the cord back, but not nearly hard enough. The mower jerked, sputtered, then settled in its stance, reluctant, unenthusiastic.

"Your hips" she coached aloud, "Flex your knees, pull with your hips."

Now she crouched slightly, hips under her shoulders, right hand clenching the handle firmly. Her eyes fixed on the mower, in one powerful move, she fired from the balls of her feet, up through her knees, her hips taking the surge and flexing her torso upright, her arm pulling the handle away from the coil. As her bicep curled, a cough followed by an eruptive growl of internal combustion expelled the blue-white smoke of success! Claire released the starter chord handle, letting it spring-rewind as she stood, fully empowered, listening to the small engine thrive with gasoline, spark and air.

She brought the paper bags meant for grass clippings into the sunlight next. Then, the plastic garbage can for the bags as they were filled. Fully prepared, Claire clasped the 'drive-lever', letting the self-propelled machine lurch forward, hungrily charging the unsuspecting grasses.

Claire guided the mower along the outer edge of the patio and to the northern fence. Turning around, she noticed the grass catcher filling quickly and returned to her starting point. Getting to within ten feet of the garbage can, she halted, the bag bulging. She lifted the back panel and pulled, straining to get the bag, corpulent with organic matter, upwards. Placing a bag in the can, she struggled briefly, needing both arms to wrestle the grass-catcher, emptying the contents in spasm-like shakes. Small bits of grass flurried about from the bag and catcher, some sticking to her forearms and neck.

Restarting the engine, she continued on a linear path to the southern fence. A quick turn and she headed back north again, trying to align this path seamlessly with the previous one; but her control wasn't enough. The mower wandered left then right, wavering under the slightest influence, letting the terrain dictate her direction. Soon so many clippings rested in the bag, the mower was overwhelmed, stalling out in the thick verdant growth.

Claire fought with all her strength to move the mower back, closer to the garbage can, lifting the swollen catcher like an unbalanced load of laundry. Once she reattached the bag, she looked about the yard. Her north-south pathways, ninety-five feet across, would be thin reductions. Each path twenty-two inches or less wide, like so many slices of cheese for approximately eighty feet downhill.

Seeing the full challenge before her, Claire stood, hands on hips, biting her lower lip a moment, "Fuck it, I'll cut it however I want."

With bag firmly attached, she yanked the mower to life and proceeded back to the south fence. A turn and forty feet more; the bag was full again. While emptying the bag, she realized the futility of trying to wipe green flecks off her skin. She stood a moment longer, her mind searching, thinking of the task, her location, the bright Saturday afternoon sunlight. Surveying her backyard and beyond, she scanned the horizon, over the fence, beyond the trees, neighbors' rooftops, everything visible to her. She again bit her lip, looked to the house, then, proclaimed, "What the hell, why not?"

Dropping the grass-catcher, she crossed her arms and clasped the hem of her tank top. In one fluid motion she lifted the top off and let it fall. Standing in the sunlight, she felt air brush the perspiration under her breasts. Nothing changed. The skies remained bright, the sun beaming omnipotently, birds still flew and no one screamed in alarm or outrage. She basked in the solar warmth bathing her, closing her eyes, smiling as a slight breeze lowered the heat awakening her chest.

Emboldened, certain of her domain, she stuck both thumbs in the waistband of her shorts. Bending and pushing down, the shorts and underwear zoomed down to her ankles. While stepping out, her left heel caught against the elasticized bands. Again, the clothes went to the ground, landing next to the tank top. Again, Claire looked to see no change in herself, the yard, her house, the neighborhood, life. Again, fresh air touched her ever so lightly, her backside, between her thighs, in simple light caresses, refreshing pores long covered, kept secret, hidden from ultra-violet and infra-red rays. Feminine hygiene might suggest protecting sensitive areas however, the immediate sense of authenticity and freedom, sensuous, intoxicating, let caution drift away with the breeze.

It started slowly, rejuvenations of mind, body and soul began flowing through Claire, joyful, a release in being, happiness. Self-confidence growing in each moment, moving her to the mower. Restarting, the mower renewed Claire's prowess, randomly walking across her lawn, looking ahead in any direction, however she deemed, delighted. Each trip around the backyard and back to the garbage can affirmed Claire's belief her life would be her own.

As she mowed, the physical strain energized her arms and legs. Descending to the eastern fence was risky, the mower's weight and mechanical drive compelling physical obedience. Taking the uphill tack challenged Claire to a forward leaning, Sisyphean conflict, controlling the machine's direction, overcoming gravity's backwards pull. The concentration needed to keep moving forward was simple, demanding, of singular purpose. Now heavy perspiration ran down her neck, her back to her tailbone, between her thighs, off breasts and down her belly, washing away frustrations, doubts, regrets. She absolved her deferential past through a five-horsepower roar, rebirthing her mystique. A moment of doubt shuddered through her, *'What if I can't finish?'*

The fury of pink panties with rhinestones sparked, her belly feeling the tinder of distrust, flashing and igniting flames of contempt for foolish women and dishonest husbands. Gripping the handle tighter, flexing her arms, bending her knees, she thrust against the resistance. Feeling gravity, weight and timidity push back against her, the tendons over her knees strained, her ankles and toes grinding, she growled, a voice gurgling from down deep as salty sweat stung her eyes. The mower started slowly, moving by inches, the powered wheels spinning against the ample grasses. Keeping her focus on the house up the incline ahead, she cajoled, *"Keep moving Claire, forward, harder."*

She roamed her grasses like a buccaneer, turning wherever, pivoting heartily. Crossing back and forth, cresting above and sinking below the green waves, every step sun washed, taking over two hours to subdue the yard to uniform height, resplendent sheen, the clean fragrance of cut grass cooling the air. Finishing her last pass along the eastern fence, Claire turned west and guided the mower laden with clippings, up the slope where the third bag waited. Letting the engine stop, completely comfortable in her shoes, sunglasses and glistening altogether, she pulled the grass-catcher one last time and being more practiced, lifted it, letting the contents rush into the paper bag. She reattached the grass-catcher to the mower and rolled them into the shed. Coming out to the waiting garbage can and bags, she stood in the sunlight, spent, aching, her body saturated. Exhilarated, she felt renewed, free of convention or care, Venus triumphant. Smiling to the sunlight she thought, *"Forty-two is nothing. I have plenty of time to be happy."*

A subtle motion to the east, just to the left, between the trees caught her eye. There, on the deck beyond the fence, standing in the sunlight, his hand shielding his eyes, Leonard Stines stood, smiling, nude.

Claire looked at the naked man one hundred and forty feet away as he viewed her. Self-aware, she was neither embarrassed nor afraid. A moment passed, then two, then three as each person stood motionless, the air moving, the sun shining, the day full. To Claire's satisfaction, she watched Leonard bring his right hand up to his right eyebrow and salute.

Claire stood fully erect, neither embarrassed nor afraid, proud, free. She took her right hand to her eyebrow, smiling as she returned the gesture. Leonard waited a moment, then turned to his waiting chaise-lounge. Collecting her shorts and top, Claire stood upright once more in the sunlight, jubilant in the moment before striding to the stairs. Bouncing up the steps she thought, *'The bags can wait. I need a shower.'*

Broken Windows, Renovated Souls

******

Three weeks later an easel stood in the center of Claire's studio, shrouded by an old, beige bed sheet. Underneath, a canvas, four feet high by five feet wide, held an image unlike anything found in any catalog or marketing or print promotional material.

The overall coloring was primarily warm, yellows, oranges, sienna's, ochres with occasional magentas and crimsons. For contrast and balance, teal blue or purple or chartreuse occasionally streaked along or nestled amongst curving lines, angled reflections, the limbs, the smile, the anatomy. A contemporary setting, poolside, having chairs, tables, some type of building and palm trees in the background. The lighting and shadows suggested midday, bright, sunny, hot but not unbearable.

There in the painting's center he lounged on a chaise, legs extended toward the viewer, a man, golden, ambered with oranges and yellows in sinewy lines, mature, sculpted, confident, nude. His eyes covered by sunglasses, he reclined, fully displayed, his muscular arms, broad-shoulders, deep chest and succulent thighs flowing to well-defined calves. The face held neither smirk nor sneer, chin slightly forward, the smile self-assured, alluring, calm, a subtle twist of confidence awaiting your response. The trim abdomen rippled down to loins where an ample, flaccid penis boldly reposed. An image surreal yet familiar, enviable maybe, compelling.

"Oh. My. Gahd." Renee chopped, beholding the image, hands close to her chest, her mouth agape, like a T-Rex stalking prey. She first moved to her right then left, starring, captivated, confessing, "I can't stop looking."

Claire asked cautiously, "Wanna show it?"

Renee snapped, "Of course I do! Do you have anything else, I mean, this is a center piece, but I hope you've got more."

"I have some others, not like this but, I could have more."

"I will give you one corner, if you can you give me six or eight more?"

"Wow, that's a lot"

"Claire, honey, if you can do this in a couple weeks, you can produce between now and June 15th, I'm sure of it."

"You think?"

"Yes, I do. You paint, I'll think, this'll be great." Renee looked to the smiling man once more, "Gahd, … he's gorgeous. You got a name for it?"

Claire put her hands behind her back and looked down, nodding her head, she softly confessed, "Relax."

Renee let the word sift through her ears as her eyes widened, her smile emerging, "Relax, that's good."

Standing up straight, Renee looked to Claire, "You'd sell this? Really?"

"Renee, a girl's gotta live."

I Spread Rocks

The doorbell chimed twice; 6:00 A.M. just as I expected. I opened the front door and there he stood. Large, tanned, sunglasses wrapping around his face, just above the cheekbones.

"Good morning, sir." His tone respectable, a practiced, professional touch.

"Good morning to you, sir," I replied.

"We here to spread the stone." He leaned back, arching slightly to his right, looking down the side of my house to the backyard area behind the gate. As he searched, he asked, "You want us to go back here?"

Opening the screen door, I stepped out and started towards the front wall corner, "Yeah, back here, the gate's unlocked."

He started walking with purpose to the metal and cedar gate standing between the front and back yards. Reaching for the latch, he opened it and walked confidently to our patio before turning left and proceeding across the patio and pool area.

"You got ten tons, right? Is that whatchoo ordered?" He proceeded all the way to the far side, some sixty-five feet and then turned at the corner. "You want it to go all the way back here?"

"Uh, no, just to where the storage box is, before the air conditioners." I stammered.

Extending his arm to his right, toward the west wall, he waved horizontally, "All out here?"

"No, no, just from where the flowers are,"

"The red ones, right?"

"Yes, the red ones and then,"

He pivoted back to me, "And then back all the way around to the gate, right?"

"Uh, yeah, back to the gate."

"Ten tons huh, that's a thousand square feet, did you measure?" He started walking toward the north wall, stepping onto the kidney-shaped space of artificial turf, the responsible grass in Arizona. I noticed his calves and their bluish-black tattoos, his dusty tan work boots, their laces flopping with each step. He looked to the areas between the privacy wall and turf and patio cement that once had held far more landscaping rocks than anyone could see now. As he bent over to look behind the Yucca plants and Pineapple palms, his faded yellow tee-shirt strained over surprisingly large back muscles, his shoulders round and full.

"And you measure this yourself, right?" He asked while scanning the dirt and rocks awaiting new covering.

"Yep, I did."

"Okay, well," He stood up and looked across the pool, back to the gate side of the yard, "We gonna start over here" he motioned to the west side, toward the air conditioners. With extended arm, his scan and sweep moved right to left as if wiping the house's entire north wall and patio area clean, "And then we work across, back over to there."

"Okay." Was my only reasonable answer.

He walked to the gate and I went back inside through the patio sliding doors. Sitting in my leather sofa, I heard muted voices and steps, starting from the street and advancing around my pool and patio apron. Quick, direct instructions in Spanish, some gestures and then the crunching rush of rocks, approximately one-inch in size, pouring from the wheel-barrows out onto the ground. The motions were straightforward, honest, efficient, it would get to 103 degrees today and certainly, no one wanted to be working under that heat.

I read the New York Times online edition, played the word scramble and mini-crossword puzzle. I tuned out the continuous efforts, from pulling stone out from the trailer bed down into the waiting wheel-barrows, the pushing of the loads across the front landscape rock to the back areas, the telltale roars of rocks being dumped and then the raking, over and over and over. The sun ascended the eastern sky, beaming omnipotently, daring anyone to view it directly.

Occasionally, I'd look out to the activity, noticing the leader sometimes shoveling, sometimes pushing a wheel-barrow, sometimes up in the trailer, bent over, pulling the ten-ton rock pile apart one shovel scoop at a time. He was in all places, doing all things and working just as hard if not harder than his three associates. There was no stopping, no brief conversations, lapses of attention, smiles or jokes shared. There was work to be done, here, before the sun could win.

Setting my coffee cup down on the table before my sofa, I looked to the clock on the bookshelf; 8:20 A.M. I heard a tapping on the patio door glass. I got up and went to see the yellow-shirted man, his face gleaming with sweat, stepping backwards, hands on hips, breathing hard while proclaiming, "Okay sir, we done, you take a look, tell me if you like."

He started walking to the west side, where the first loads fell. I followed as he spoke, "We put it over here like you said." He then proceeded to lead me all around the pool apron, along the north wall, letting me examine the product of labor. Arriving at the eastern side of the pool, he looked back, first towards the red flowers and then to the turf area, my three-dozen or so golf balls shining in the sunlight, the practice net sagging from its six-by-eight-foot frame as a morning breeze waffled through it.

"Looks good to me" I answered, "Really good."

"Yeah?"

"Yeah, I watched through the windows earlier, you were all working and I liked what I saw." I smiled briefly, my reflection distorted in his sunglasses, giving me a strange orange-yellow face.

"Thank you," he replied. He pointed to the practice net, "That's a nice net you got there. You play a lot?"

"Nah, not that much anymore." I sheepishly admitted.

"No? I started playing a couple years ago. I dunno, sometimes I hit pretty good; sometimes it feels good to just bash the shit outta the ball, you know?" He rubbed his chin and jaw, his fingers large, calloused and muscled from pulling, grasping, working.

I stopped for a moment, tilting my head down slightly, then looked up to him, "About, lemme see, fifty-eight years ago, I was a caddy at a country club. This one doctor came and played two or three times a week and he always had me caddy for him. He told me one day 'Georgie, I can teach you how to play this game in thirty minutes and you'll spend the rest of your life trying to get it right.'"

"Huh-heaw" he laughed, a smile breaking broadly across his face as he lifted the brim of his straw hat off his brow, "That's about right!" He chuckled twice more and then asked me, "So, what do you do now?"

"Oh, I'm retired." I replied, my voice fading in the last syllable.

"What did you do?"

"I was a lawyer."

"Huh." He looked to the western sky, "You seem pretty nice for a lawyer."

I looked at this man, a stranger two hours ago, now complimenting me. I'd watched his leadership, his effort, skills and energy on a Sunday morning, working when many people were sipping coffee, eating breakfast, thinking of doing nothing. He stood proud, portraying a special nobility and dignity in his willingness to do what others would not. Then, in a softer voice he asked, "You got any kids?"

"Oh yeah, and grandkids." I smiled.

"I got kids. I dunno, they don't seem to understand." He looked again to the horizon beyond my privacy wall, "They think money just comes off trees or something."

I nodded in agreement, "Yeah, now that mine are grown and got kids; they see things differently."

His head bobbed up and down, "Yeah! Yeah, it's different when you got mouths to feed. Then you gotta do something." He stood still, hands still on his hips, breathing easier, looking, searching. He turned to me, "Well, thank you sir, thanks for the work." He paused a moment and then asked, "You were a lawyer huh?"

"Yeah, yeah I was." I too looked to the western horizon, "A long time ago."

He shrugged his shoulders and stuck out his hand to shake, "I spread rocks."

Dixie Cup

"RANDY!! RANDY!!"

A smaller boy ran down the sidewalk, turning into the driveway where adults stood, drinking, laughing, smoking. Weaving through twenty or so people, the boy found his older brother sitting on an aluminum folding chair in the single car garage, behind a wooden pic-nic table and various chairs. Breathless, his cheeks wet, his tee-shirt stained, dusty jeans and dirty Chuck Taylors', one shoe lace dangerously extended, he stopped two feet from three teenage boys, holding plastic cups filled with beer from the keg they guarded. Laughing, they paid the lad no attention.

"RANDY!! Dad says come home, now!"

"WHY?!" the seventeen-year-old snarled, eyes flashing under sandy-brown hair, daring the little boy to respond. He stood up, his five-foot nine-inch frame, still adolescent in body mass, still younger than appeared, looking directly to the smaller brother standing his ground, just as defiant, "It's about Michael, Dad says come home now."

Randy Timmerman's face softened, casting his eyes down to an oil stain under the pic-nic table. His beer was holding off heartbreak and he wasn't drunk enough yet to be healed. The first Saturday in

June and friend Kenny Hoslin's older sister, Kathie, married "Dave", ending Randy's dream of wooing and bedding Kathie. Her being three years older didn't matter, if Randy believed one thing true; he believed his desire could overcome any obstacle.

"Randy, c'mon, right now." Markie, Randy's ten-year old brother now stood close, his arms and hands waving, emphasizing his paternal fear. Taking a long, full gulp of beer, Randy held the cup up, his index finger extended, telling Markie to hold still as his ballooned cheeks slowly deflated. Swallowing, he turned to his closest friend Joey Walsh, "Come with me,"

Equal to Randy in height and frame, Joey finished his beer and followed the Timmerman boys down the driveway. The trio walked down the sidewalk past single-story ranch-style houses, the afternoon sunlight showing newer paint from the old. The Timmerman house held neighborhood prominence through its stylish brick half-wall under fashionable avocado-green shiplap siding. The oversized two-car garage was connected by the aluminum breezeway spanning from the house. Black trimmed windows and gutters under a charcoal grey roof provided admirable contrast to the evergreens and flower beds Mrs. Timmerman tended like the intensive care nurse she once was.

Stopping at the curb, Randy and Joey viewed the olive-drab Ford sedan parked directly in front of the house. After looking both ways Markie crossed, but the older boys slowed under a heaviness in anticipation of whatever awaited. As Markie walked up the narrow side walk to the front stoop, Randy first, then Joey, walked to the space between the house and garage, taking their usual entry through the kitchen door.

They passed through the kitchen, over the dining room shag carpeting, toward the living room, their gait slowing as wails, sobs, agony and pain swirled about, washing each person. Dale, Ruth, oldest daughter Terry, an Army officer sitting in one of the swivel chairs, brother Robbie and brother Tommy, rubbing his eye with a fist as he cried into Terry's chest. Walking past the dining table the boys stopped, gawking at the room of despair. Ruth Timmerman's body slumped to her left, into Dale's chest, his right arm across her back, bouncing with the quakes she couldn't control. Robbie, the softest of the boys, sat in a gold velour swivel chair, bent at his waist, arms folded across his lap, his puffy cheeks, dappled with red blotches almost swallowing his red-rimmed eyes, "Randy," he pleaded, "Michael's not coming home from Viet Nam."

Randy looked to his father Dale; his black-rimmed glasses pushed up on his forehead as he wiped his eyes with a red-paisley handkerchief. A plumber by trade, Dale was a no-nonsense father, strong, physically and mentally. But now, sitting in his white overalls and blue work-shirt, he sobbed uncontrollably, his chest heaving as he gasped for air, his despair the loudest of all. Randy struggled to understand, "What'dya mean?"

Terry looked to him, her eyes red, her nose redder, especially at the tip, "He went on a mission Tuesday, his chopper went down, they haven't found him yet."

Randy stiffened, his chest started heaving up and down, his fingers wiggled slightly as he watched his mother, father, sister, brothers; it was too much, too much today. Turning abruptly, he went back through the kitchen, hitting the aluminum screen door with such force, it locked open. His teenage frame, all one-hundred forty pounds bounced down the two concrete steps as Joey followed him out to the garage. Standing in the doorway, Randy doubled over, hands over his ears, "EEEAAAUUUGGGHHHH" roared up from his twisted body.

As the agony left his lungs and flowed onto the concrete floor, Randy stood and quickly grabbed a large pipe wrench, thirty-six inches long, hoisting it above his head like a lumberjack. Down at an angle it quickly came, striking one of two mounted snow tires leaning against the wall. The impact made the tire jump as the wrench rebounded, a thud sending the wrench head back to Randy's shoulders. Infuriated, Randy recoiled his slight frame and swung again, harder. Another bounce, another tire hop, another louder thud. Now the rage was uncontainable, the rebound inertia pulled Randy further left, his emotions overwhelming him. From his toes he pulled all the strength he could find and swung the ten-pound wrench so hard his feet left the floor. Down came the jaws and head, the angle even lower, just below shoulder level, striking the fully inflated truck tire sidewall.

"EEAAUUGGHH" Randy again vented, eyes tear-filled, blurred, unfocused. The wrench hit the sidewall flat with such force the recoil shot the tool back from Randy's grip. Flying away loose, it careened three feet into the driver's door window and outer rearview mirror of his mother's prized 1969 Aqua Marine Lincoln Continental. The window exploded into hundreds of small pieces, spraying across the interior, bench seat, dash panel, floor carpets, up into the defroster vents under the windshield as the rearview mirror fell to the garage floor. His face white and puffy, blue eyes glistening, Randy looked to Joey. Joey bit his lower lip and started walking toward the Lincoln.

Randy slowly descended into a crouching ball, crying, moaning at first before howling, "Why? Why isn't Michael here? I want him to come home." Placing his head between his knees, he let his sorrow and pain flow through his body out to the floor.

"What the hell happened IN HERE?!" Dale's voice suddenly boomed. The boys stiffened; a day that couldn't possibly get any worse just did. Dale walked directly to the car door, past two boys now fearing for their lives. Looking in through the window cavity for a moment, he pulled his head back and without standing erect, looked down to Randy, "Jesus Christ! What the hell'd you do boy?"

******

"So, you'll start Wednesday afternoon, just three or four hours, we'll show you around, you can start on the register first, Friday night, Saturday and Sunday."

Randy nodded obediently, watching the older, silver-haired man standing behind the counter. Arlen Klaeckert, son of Gustavus, founder of Klaeckert's Hardware, leaned on the counter top, a cigarette between his fingers waving smoke as he wrote on Randy's employment application, "You'll start at a dollar sixty-five per hour and we'll see how it goes, Okay?"

Standing upright, Arlen took a drag off his cigarette and as streams of smoke flowed down from his nostrils, he offered, "Tell your Mom and Dad we're really sorry about your brother." Recalling last Saturday's scene, Randy looked to the countertop and nodded silently.

Klaeckert's Hardware was *the* source for local building trades, from larger builders, plumbers and electrical companies to individual contractors. The original store front was the main entry into the expansive hardware oasis, requiring patrons to take three stairs up to the main floor, then down a five-foot wide hardwood aisle, the widest in the whole complex, to the one and only cash register. A National Register Model No.9901, twenty-inches tall, two feet wide, weighing almost fifty pounds, an engraved brass exterior, its key tabs were 5/8" in diameter. Pushing them down required strength and determination to cause the 2-inch numeral tabs to appear between the glass panels at the top. An operator could develop Popeye-like forearms working this register day after day.

The counter was six feet wide and three feet deep, a dark, hardwood top over an originally white base, rumored to have once been a local synagogue altar; but no one was certain. Directly behind the counter was Gustavus Klaeckert's famous declaration; *'If we don't have it; you don't need it.'*

It was in this storied labyrinth of fasteners, tubing, chains, nails, paint, thinner, cheese cloth packets, saws, hammers, sandpaper and myriad other implements of manual labor and artisan craftsmanship Randy Timmerman started his road to Damascus. Standing behind the counter Wednesday night around 6:20 p.m., Randy tried to be industrious and straighten the many little things laying casually about the counter top. Note pads, three pencils, a stapler, two tape measures (one six-foot, one twelve-foot), a weathered four-ounce, white Dixie cup, having small green leaves just around its circumference beneath the lip, some paper clips, a utility knife and a glass cutter amongst other tools of hardware store trade.

Wiping off the dust, Randy aligned the pencils, cutter and knife, putting them alongside the stapler. He lifted the Dixie cup, looking inside, it was empty, holding some dust in the base seam, he turned to toss it into the trashcan behind him.

"Don't touch that!" A voice called from down an aisle to the south side of the store. The sound of feet shuffling across the hardwood floor grew louder as a stout, older man appeared, "That's mine, leave it alone."

Randy looked at the shorter man, standing directly before him, his plain grey glasses frames held lenses with visible bifocal sections, smudged by fingers, cigarette smoke and time. Although it was June, he wore a flannel, long-sleeved shirt, his white tee-shirt visible underneath. His shirt's pocket lined with a white plastic sleeve holding a six-inch stainless-steel ruler, two mechanical pencils and a clear Bic pen. Silver-dark hair was neatly parted on one side, just like his mother taught him decades ago. Tan suspenders with brass clasps held blue-denim work pants, belted and cuffed to reveal their telltale red-plaid flannel lining, buckling against Redwing half-boots. His face almost round, his physique sagged a bit, his back starting to curl forward. His fingers were thick, like sausages, capable of gripping and never weakening.

"Just put it back, I'll take care of it." The man asserted, "You must be the new kid,"

Randy nodded as he gently guided the cup back to its original spot. Once settled, he stepped back, wiping his hands on the back of his jeans. If Randy didn't know what to expect, the man removed any doubt, "You're here to run the register right?"

Again, Randy nodded, he'd never seen this person before. Now this flannelled mogul was telling him in no uncertain language his role. Cautiously, Randy asked, "Who are you?"

"I'm Dixie, I work here." He proceeded around the counter and back to a single metal stool, next to the fire extinguisher. Stepping on the ring that stabilized the legs, he pulled himself up to sit, turned and wedged his back against the partial chair back about six inches above the seat. He fit the seat like it was built for him, or he for it, Randy couldn't tell. Reaching into his shirt pocket, he pulled a pack of cigarettes out. Randy recognized the maroon packaging of Pall-Mall's, the only cigarettes without filters.

Dixie pulled a cigarette out from the packet's bottom, keeping it secured between his index and thumb fingernails, inserting the other end precisely in the corner of his lips. Next, he withdrew a silver cigarette lighter. Popping it open, he lit the cigarette, inhaling deeply as he returned the cigarettes and lighter to his pocket, smoke flowed evenly from his nostrils towards the counter. Sitting upright on the stool, he quietly smoked while Randy wondered what he should talk about? He didn't have to think for long; Dixie calmly asked, "So, why're you working here kid?"

"I kinda busted up my mom's car, gotta pay

for the repairs."

"Busted up?" His arms crossing his chest, Dixie leaned slightly forward, hands tucked in opposite armpits.

"Yeah, I was mad, I really fucked up."

Staring up at the fluorescents, Dixie let his eyes work across from left to right, then asked the ceiling, "Did you fuck up? Or just screw up?"

Randy paused, repeating the words, one by one, his mind trying to discern the difference. He turned to face Dixie, "What'dya mean?"

The older man's eyes came to Randy's as his right hand removed the cigarette from his lips, "It's simple; a screw up you can fix: a fuck up you can't do nuthin' about."

Leaning back against the National, Randy looked to the floor. Dixie sat on his stool, staring ahead to the store front doors. Slowly, Randy's head started nodding, not lifting his face, he peered up, "I guess I just screwed up, cause Rollins Ford is going to fix it, but I have to pay for it. I had a bad day, a girl I liked got married and my brother got killed in Viet Nam."

Dixie sat still, both hands on his knees, watching Randy. As tears grew in Randy's eyes, Dixie looked to the storefront, "Jesus kid, I guess you did have a bad day."

Broken Windows, Renovated Souls

******

The Saturday business was brisk, steady and mildly entertaining to Randy, Arlen and Dixie. Randy arrived at eight-thirty a.m., a half-hour before the store opened, to find Arlen and Dixie behind the counter, drinking coffee, eating donuts. The donuts were a Saturday fixture of Arlen's, he never ate lunch, choosing a donut about every three hours all day. They were relaxed, laughing, talking, gearing up for a busy day. And busy it was; Arlen sold two riding lawn mowers, maybe three hundred pounds of fertilizer, planting soil or compost material.

Dixie cut and mounted six window panes, broken by one thing or another. Shortly after one o'clock, a customer asked Randy where the hammers were?

"Follow me, I'll show you," he offered, only to hear Dixie behind him, "You handle the register, I'll help the customer."

Randy watched as Dixie walked by without ever looking at him, "Hammers? One, two?"

"Ah, just one I guess." The man's face opened as he showed

his naivete.   Holding a small piece of paper in his fingers, he followed Dixie to the aisle, stepping cautiously behind the flannel and suspenders. Randy heard Dixie's next question rise over the shelves, "Claw hammer? Framing? What kind?" A mumbled response, indiscernible, fell to the hardwood floor somewhere between the aisles.

Through the building acquisitions, years of use, changes in hardware retailing, the store's aisles and shelving configurations changed, only the hardwood flooring being an original fixture. Keeping Gus' mantra of having everything needed as the guiding light, updated shelving, upright racks, peg-board walls, all bearing everything and anything ever made in the hardware universe brought about a most unusual phenomenon; other than the main entry aisle, no aisle was more than three feet wide, making the store a labyrinth beyond anything Theseus could have imagined.

Many a customer frightened, lost, had called from somewhere between some aisles, panicked by packages of screws, nuts, washers, garden tools, furnace filters, paint brushes or other monsters of suburban maintenance.

Dixie knew every aisle, every step, every location for any product. Sometimes, if a customer was irritable or rude, Dixie would lead them one way to their product, show it to them and then quickly disappear through the maze, leaving the boor to fend for himself. Once they returned to the counter, they'd find Dixie, seated on his stool, smiling sardonically as their transaction was completed.

It was about four o'clock that Saturday when Randy saw another side of Dixie. The bells over the door signaled three young men entering the store, walking to the counter. Randy instantly recognized two of them; Dominic Palumbo and younger brother Vincent, sons of Argento Palumbo, owner of Palumbo Tile and Flooring. They attended St. Patrick's Elementary when Michael, Randy and Robbie were students.

Just over six-foot two, Dominic took great pains to keep his jet-black hair meticulously coifed, his pompadour rising perfectly but for one rebellious single curled strand, returning everyone's sight to his pale blue eyes. His complexion smooth and clear, having no marks, blemishes or acne. He became fond of bench presses and E-Z bar curls and favored sleeveless T-shirts showing his biceps, chest, chest hairs and gold crucifix. Vincent was not so impressive, topping out at five-foot six, no shoulders, a torso resembling a football. 'Vinnie' as he was known, wasn't as genetically fortunate. Beside his corpulence, his facial complexion displayed an ongoing struggle between blackheads, pimples and random wiry black hairs.

Dominic spoke evenly; Vinnie tended to use words like quick, short, repetitive jabs. If they could be thought of as dogs; Dominic was a Rottweiler; Vinnie a chubby terrier.

As the trio approached the counter, Dominic started, "Uh, yeah, I need some nuts and washers." He held a small piece of white paper, looking at it once more as Vinnie echoed, "yeah, nuts and washers." Looking up, Dominic saw Randy and smiled, "Hey, don't I know you?"

"Yeah," Randy nodded, gulping slightly. Randy remembered an afternoon at Warren Park. Taller for his age, Dominic entertained himself sometimes by walking behind the swings, the long, chained, hard rubber sling seated swings that little kids loved. When they swung backwards, Dominic grabbed the chains, stopping their motion, holding the children aloft. Sometimes, depending on how loud they screamed, he'd lift them higher, raising the seat over his head, mercilessly terrorizing 1st and 2nd graders. Michael Timmerman was Dominic's 6th grade classmate and practicing Little League baseball with his team about one-hundred feet away. Robbie, a second-grader, screamed in abject terror from his swing seat and Michael looked to find his little brother. Seeing Dominic's upright arms and Robbie squirming and screaming, Michael sprinted from third base, directly to Robbie's rescue. It took him maybe ten seconds, Michael yelling, "Let him go Dominic!"

Dominic paid no attention; Vinnie's eyes bulged as if his head suddenly inflated. Watching from a pic-nic table by the water fountain, Randy got up and ran to the swings also, arriving seconds later. "Dominic! Put him down!" Michael yelled. Dominic sneered, "What'ya gonna do?"

"Yeah! What'ya gonna do?" Vinnie chimed.

Michael came up to Dominic and with one short, lightning quick punch, struck him in the center of his chest. Falling backwards, Dominic released the swing, freeing a crying Robbie. Dominic landed on his back and buttocks before pushing himself up. Standing with mouth open, wide eyed, Vinnie watched. Dominic rushed Michael, trying to wrap his arms around Michael's, hoping to bind against more punches. The boys fell to the ground, twisting sideways, giving Michael opportunity to land on top. Sitting on Dominic's chest, Michael grabbed Dominic's wrists, "I don't want to fight you! Just leave the little kids alone!"

Michael pushed Dominic's arms above his head, pinning him to the ground, dirt sticking to Dominic's carefully combed, Vitalis gleaming hair. Firmly under Michael's control, Dominic's red cheeks threatened, "You better hope I don't get up!"

"I'm gonna get up Dom, I'm gonna let you up and this'll be over, understand?"

Dominic waited, his eyes looking around to either side, wondering who was watching, before he nodded. Michael looked directly into Dominic's eyes, "Okay, I'm gonna get up, this is over between us, right?"

The dusty head with shiny hair nodded once more. Michael released the wrists, putting his hands on his thighs to get up and relieve the pressure from Dominic's abdomen. Michael bent down and retrieved his baseball glove, a Spaulding Minnie Minoso model the entire sixth grade envied. Michael stood up just in time to see Vinnie rushing at him, his right arm gripping a metal lunch box cocked behind his head, tears streaming down his cheeks. Vinnie spat, "Son-of-a-bitch!"

As the arm came forward, bringing down the metal box, Michael reflexively shot his glove hand up. The impact destabilized Vinnie, causing his hand and lunch box to bounce back directly, striking Vinnie's right cheek, knocking him close to Dominic, now sitting on the ground trying to hide his embarrassment. The lunchbox struck Vinnie's cheek, just below his right eye, hard enough to create purple-blue-olive-yellow discoloring that lasted almost two weeks. For the last weeks of school, Vinnie suffered jeers and taunts for having given himself a black-eye with his lunch box. Dominic Palumbo went on being difficult to some students, but he never crossed another Timmerman boy. Leaning on the counter, Dominic smiled, "You're Timmerman, right?"

Randy stood erect behind the register, "Yeah, I'm Randy."

"Right" Dominic smiled, "How's your brother Mike, I heard he went in the Army?"

"He's dead."

Dominic's face dropped the smile as his head snapped back, like having been slapped. Stepping to one side, Dominic looked to the counter, "Oh yeah, what happened? He get shot or sumthin'?"

In one step, Dixie came off the stool, his knuckles coming to the countertop, arms slightly forward, wider than shoulder width, ready to launch. Randy noticed the hairs on the back of Dixie's neck standing straight up, like Mrs. Cook's Airedale "Roxy" whenever anybody rang her doorbell. The move startled the four boys. "What difference does it make?" Dixie growled, "He's dead, show some respect."

The air went stale, no one moving, no one blinking. Finally, Dixie stepped back, "What're you here for?"

Dominic watched Dixie, "I need some 'C- nuts' and 'L- washers'."

Dixie's brow knitted, then he started walking from behind the counter, "Come with me."

As Dixie shuffled off, the three watched a moment more before following. Seeing the direction the group headed, Randy recognized Dixie's taking the long, confusing route to the fastener aisle. Four minutes later Dixie returned, taking his post on the stool. He and Randy listened to the three voices, coming closer, then drifting off, arguing, moving, finally arriving at the counter almost ten minutes later. Randy rang up the one-dollar and nineteen cent transaction, making change for two singles. Dixie remained stone-faced, staring out to the street, his hands tucked in his armpits, a cigarette smoldering between his lips. As the door swung closed behind the Palumbo brothers, Randy asked, "Take em' on an adventure Dixie?"

Dixie never moved, "I've had to deal with them and their old man for years. They don't respect nothing. Little pricks."

******

Walking through the stale heat of a late June afternoon, Randy recognized his good fortune working in an air-conditioned store. He pulled the door open, the bells jangling loudly, ascended the three steps and headed down the aisle toward the counter. It was 3:45 p.m. and he would take his position manning the National promptly at four o'clock, just as scheduled. Nearing the counter, he saw Arlen standing, reading something, his cigarette signaling from between his right index and middle fingers. Once Randy was within four feet, Arlen looked up, "Hello Randy, go punch in," Arlen smiled, "Then we'll talk."

Randy let Arlen's words sink in, this was different from the daily, hardware store routine.

"I'll need you to work here Wednesday, Thursday and Friday nights until Fourth of July week. Is that gonna be okay with your parents?"

Randy was at first annoyed by Arlen's suggestion he needed his parent's permission to work. Waiting a moment to think he shrugged, "Nah, It'll be fine, my Mom wants the Lincoln fixed right away."

Arlen chuckled, "I'll bet she does." Leafing through the newspaper, Arlen asked, "So how's it going with Dixie?"

Randy stood silent, looking to Arlen, trying to understand. Arlen snorted suddenly, the cigarette smoke entering the wrong way, "You look surprised?"

Randy searched his mind, "Well, he's kind of, uhm, … pretty straight-forward, you know?"

Arlen listened closely, the paper in his right hand, he tucked it up under his left armpit, taking the cigarette out and exhaling slowly. Turning his back to the storefront, he leaned against the countertop and looked to the ceiling, "Yeah, well, there's a lot people don't know, a lot more to Brian Corcoran than you see."

"Brian?"

Arlen turned to Randy, looking down, putting the cigarette back for one last drag, "You didn't know that was his name?"

Randy shook his head, trying to recall ever hearing anyone, customer, friend or acquaintance, utter that name, "No, never."

Recalling a fond memory, Arlen's smile crept out, "Brian and Brendan Corcoran, they were a pair."

"Brendan?" Another completely unknown name.

"His twin brother, older by twenty-five minutes."

"An older twin brother?" Randy's head was swirling.

"Yep, in high school the Corcoran boys were something. Redheaded, neither taller than five-foot four, ever. Took all kinds of crap for being short, redheaded, fatherless, sooner or later they fought every boy." Arlen rubbed out the cigarette butt in the stamped metal ashtray. That's when Randy noticed the cup's absence, "So, what's with his little white cup?"

Arlen looked to the same spot, visualizing the cup's presence. Stepping to the stool, Arlen sat down, his eyes searching beyond the store windows, out faraway. "Brendan and Brian graduated, June, 1943. The next week they enlisted in the Army Air Corps. Marie, their mother, was beside herself." Arlen paused, recalling the mother's forlorn eyes, her resigned posture, powerless once again. "Because they were so short, they both became belly gunners."

Randy squinted, another name or term he'd never heard before. Seeing Randy's squint, Arlen came back to the present, "Bombers, B-17's and B-24's, had these polyurethane ball-shaped turrets about three feet in diameter that hung below the plane, on its 'belly'. Short guys were trained to get in, crouched up like a baby, and shoot two

.50 caliber machine guns. Once in the air, other crewmen would close the hatch, lock it, and crank the ball down into position, letting it turn freely, 360 degrees, to shoot any Germans trying to shoot down their plane."

Now Randy began to see, "In a plastic ball? Sheeeiit."

"Gets pretty damn cold at 25,000 feet altitude. Each crew member took his own little cup with him on every flight. If he was wounded and bleeding, his blood would freeze into little pellets, they'd tried to collect them in the cup, to take back and use in the hospital."

"Did Dixie use his?"

"I don't know, I never asked." Arlen looked back to the windows, "He and his brother trained together, ate together, did everything together until it came for their overseas assignments. They thought they'd figured out the sequencing and spaced themselves in line. Brian miscounted and went one space too far; Brendan went to Libya with a B-24 crew and Brian got sent to England with a new B-17 crew."

Randy's head sunk down, chin almost touching his chest, remembering a time he and Michael got separated at scout camp; terrifying Randy, "Gawd, that's terrible."

"That's not the worst," Arlen continued, "Brian and his crew went on some of the most dangerous missions, getting Europe ready for D-Day, seeing other planes blown out of the sky, trying to survive twenty-five missions so they could come home."

Now the story consumed Arlen, flowing from his mind and heart, resurrecting some grief he'd held for a friend. Letting words roll forward, his lips enunciated precisely, cleansing his soul, "Brian's ship lost two engines, part of a wing and part of the tail. The captain, left the formation, going down to like 10,000 feet, bringing a bunch of fighters with. There was a small fire in the radio hold, they were leaking fuel, so the captain ordered everyone to bail out. He was trying to get over the channel and when he did, he wanted every man jumping. That's when Brian's troubles started."

Arlen's eyelids flitted, like the frames of an old newsreel, a new cigarette between his fingers.Enthralled, Randy's eyes lifted up from the countertop, he asked, "What happened?"

"The other three gunners tried raising the ball turret, only to discover pieces of shrapnel had broken and jammed the gears. The latch had been hit too, welding the lock mechanism, trapping Brian in the ball. True to their pact, the three sat down inside the plane, just above Brian, where he could see them. For almost twenty minutes they stayed there while German fighters fed on the B-17." Arlen put the cigarette to his lips, holding it as he inhaled, letting a moment pass before geysers of smoke left his nostrils flowing downward, down to his thighs and knees.

"When the ship got ready hit the water, two fighters passed

over, almost every round striking the wings and fuselage. A fuel-cell exploded and the plane flopped down the last twenty-five feet, breaking in half when it hit." Arlen brought the heels of his palms together, "The nose and tail sections pointed up, making a V-shape. The impact broke the ball turret loose, but the three gunners went under with the tail. The entire aircraft sank in less than a minute. Brian was stuck in the ball, like a big bobber, rising up to the surface, bouncing on the water."

Now, Arlen stopped talking, pulling off his glasses and pinching the bridge of his nose. Randy tried to mentally picture floating in a plastic ball, watching your plane sink in some ocean. The image frightened him immediately, making him shudder hard against the countertop. When the silence no longer felt heavy, Arlen's fatherly voice concluded, "So, September, 1943, Brendan and Brian Corcoran left America and in November, 1944, Dixie Cup came home. Two eighteen-year-old boys left; one old man came back."

Arlen stared at the storefront, the daylight of 4:45 tinged with orange. Randy wondered who this man he thought he knew really was? A question popped to mind, *'What about Brendan?'*

Arlen finished his story, "About the time Brian went on that mission, Brendan's plane went missing over North Africa. Convinced he jinxed Brendan, Brian said he fucked up, killed his brother."

******

"Mary Anne,"

The voice stirred Randy's mind, away from the open sea, away from the sail boat he found himself standing on, under clouds, the sun peeping through in single, random rays. Comfortable, warm, not wanting to awaken, Randy hoped to see Michael standing next to him again, he'd been right there just a moment earlier.

Rolling up from his slumber to see only the ceiling of his bedroom, Randy looked quickly to the single window, the sunrise lighting the neighborhood air in pinks and oranges and yellows, a lighter blue rising above to darker night air. Leaning up on one arm, he waited, trying to be certain where he was. It was his bedroom, the bed he laid on last night, the room he'd shared with Michael all his life, the safest, quietest bedroom. Now, it was different, lonely, a place to change clothes, sleep in and avoid for fear of memories of boyish pranks and late-night talks. He asked the sunrise softly, "Michael? Is that you?"

Putting on denim cutoff shorts and a tee shirt, Randy quietly opened his bedroom door, looking down the hallway to his brother's bedrooms, their doors closed, the house silent. Carefully stepping down the stairway, he walked to the kitchen where he discovered Dale casually smoking a cigarette, reading the newspaper, a single cup of black coffee on the small glass-topped patio table.

"Oh, hey Dad, what're you doing up?"

"I'm always up by now, what're you doing up?" Dale took a slow drag from his cigarette. Sitting down to the table, Randy scratched his head, his eyes blinking, "Uhm, do you ever dream something about someone and it holds you, like you can't think of anything else?"

"You have a bad dream son?"

Randy sat for a moment, thinking about what he thought he saw, felt, heard, "It wasn't bad; it was weird. Michael was with me; I think."

Dale looked up through the black rimmed glasses, his cigarette smoking from the corner of his lips, "Michael?"

"Yeah, we were walking, or I was, but it felt like he was with me." A yawn started opening Randy's mouth, expanding his face, teeth showing, "We were, ... uh, walking across town, then, standing by this big sailboat, like the ones on Lake Michigan you know?"

Watching his son, Dale nodded slightly, the paper limp in his hands.

"Then, at the sailboat, I couldn't see Michael anymore, but I heard, 'Mary Anne', and then I woke up. You ever have that happen?"

Dale cleared his throat, after sipping his coffee he asked, "What do you think it means?"

"I don't know. I felt completely calm, I wasn't afraid or nothing. I wonder why he said, 'Mary Anne'? Do you think he meant his girlfriend Mary Anne?"

"I don't know son, it's your dream."

"Should I ask Mom? She always talks about stuff like this."

"Not today son, she's gonna have enough to handle without your dream."

Michael Timmerman's body arrived at O'Hare Airport on Tuesday night and was transported to Daugherty's Funeral Home on Wednesday morning. Later that afternoon, Dale went to view his son's body, a last look at his nineteen-year-old boy, a decorated combat veteran, not old enough to buy liquor or vote, just old enough to die. A veteran himself, Dale went alone fearing their son's final version might forever damage his wife's memories. His suspicions were correct, the opened casket revealed a damaged, incomplete body in dress uniform, ribbons and badges and a nameplate declaring 'Timmerman'. Returning home, Dale forsook dinner and spent the night sitting on his patio, drinking Jack Daniel's sour mash deep into the darkness.

Now, Thursday, the family visitation would start this evening at five o'clock; the general visitation at six. People started arriving at 5:45, lining up outside, patiently, politely respecting the family's time. People dressed in darker colors, suits, some ladies wearing hats and gloves, all speaking in hushed tones, some men standing to one side, smoking, talking quietly, swiftly, exhaling and shaking their heads under murmurs of, "it's a damn shame, a goddamn shame."

Daugherty's had one main receiving room, a large rectangular space, two different double doored entries, soft-hued wallpaper and light brown carpeting. A hundred or so wooden folding chairs having plush upholstered seats were standing and people sat in random groups after passing the closed casket. The line of mourners snaked along the far wall all the way to the back wall, then along and bending back to the first entry. From that point the line meandered slightly in small groups of two or three people all the way out of the lobby and double glass doors to the parking lot.

Sitting in the anteroom, the Timmerman children all took seats behind a sofa that faced the main room, opposite the casket stand; the floral arrangements provided a barrier from those paying their last respects. Two bi-folding louvered doors were drawn back, giving the children a full view of the line as it proceeded from the entry doors to the main room.

"Randy, look at all these people" Markie whispered, his eyes searching, "Who are they?"

"Friends of Mom and Dad's, kids from school, people who work with Dad."

"Who's that man, over there in the black suit?"

"Which one?"

"The tall man, see, with the woman in the blue dress and hat,"

"The Mayor," Randy whispered.

"That's the *mayor*?" Markie's surprise raised his voice.

"Sshhh, keep it down, yeah, he's the mayor."

Looking a little further beyond the mayor's position, Randy spied familiar figures; Mary Anne Bonavia and her parents.Standing patiently, Mary Anne, her father Pete and mother Marie were all dressed in black, Mary Anne and Marie each wearing a black lace handkerchief clipped to their hair with a bobby-pin. Mary Anne was Michael's girlfriend; his fiancé when he left for Viet Nam.

Randy had long envied his brother's good fortune in finding Mary Anne, she was by every description angelic. Her light complexion was framed by strawberry blond hair, her figure shapely, not yet mature but womanly. Her hands were dainty, her nails perfectly manicured. When she ate with the Timmerman family at Sunday dinner, her manners were perfect, her voice soft, she smiled, beaming whenever Michael spoke. Even from this distance, Randy noticed her cheeks reddened, swollen, her eyes puffy, her posture forlorn.

"Randy" Ruth's voice called, "Go get Mary Anne and her parents, tell them to come up here."

Dutifully, Randy stood and walked directly to them, "My mom says you should come up with us."

Waiting a moment, Mary Anne stood to one side as her father and mother stepped out of line and started walking to the anteroom. Walking behind them, she looked to Randy, her eyes rimmed red, her nostrils also cherry-colored.

"Hey Mary Anne,"

"Hi, Randy, how are you?"

Randy couldn't answer, he hadn't thought of how or what to feel, this setting being unlike anything he ever knew. He scrambled to respond and blustered, "Oh, I don't know, I keep looking at that box and," his voice drifted away.

Mary Anne started quaking, her hand coming to her nose as she leaned over to Randy's shoulder. Instinctively, he put his arm across her, feeling her body sag into his side, shaking, her crying muffled by his jacket. As they entered the room, Randy saw his mother and

Marie embracing one another, holding each other as their bodies shook, weeping in unison. Peter and Dale shook hands; their free hands on each other's shoulders. The future joys of both families all gone, painfully lost.

Breaking the embrace, Marie offered, "I left some lasagna and wine at the house."

"Oh Marie, you shouldn't have,"

"Sshh, sshh, you don't need to be cooking right now. You need anything, *anything* Ruth, you call me, you hear?" Marie stared into Ruth's teary eyes, her chin quivering, she softly begged, "What am I going to do Marie? They killed my baby."

Holding Mary Anne, Randy looked to his father, his eyes now streaming tears as Pete consoled, "It's a goddamn shame Dale, he didn't deserve this. Michael was a good kid, kid, hell, he was a good man, I don't care how old, he's a hero, you know?"

Dale nodded, his lips blubbering under tears and alcohol, his body appearing less solid, less certain. Randy looked down to Mary Anne watching the adults, tears silently streaming down her cheeks too. Looking to Randy, Mary Anne asked, "Can I tell you something?"

"Sure,"

She looked out to the hallway, "Let's go out there,"

They turned, his arm relaxing from her shoulders, she walked to a small alcove holding two chairs and small table, a box of Kleenex standing guard. Looking at the people still lining up, quietly waiting, she paused, "Do you think people, people you don't know, can talk to you, in your sleep?"

Randy's face opened, his eyes growing wide as he considered the question, "What'ya mean?"

"Last night, I had a dream," she looked around again, "I was walking down a street, I don't know where I was, but I was scared, I wanted to get home, but I couldn't find a way."

"Yeah?"

"And then, this short man, in like an Army uniform, but from like, those war movies, you know, World War Two, he said, 'Come with me' and I went with him."

Randy was curious, bringing his hands to his hips, "Okay,"

Then we were somewhere, there was this big sailboat, you know, like the ones sailing on the ocean?" A chill crossed Randy's spine, his eyes locked on Mary Anne's as he remembered his dream, "Then what happened?"

"The short man said, 'Tell my brother, Brendan says it's okay."

"Brendan?"

Mary Anne shook her head as her chin trembled, "I don't know, I don't know any Brendan. Then, I heard Michael's voice, he said

'Mary Anne, I love you."

Tears began filling Mary Anne's eyes as Randy's stomach turned, his head spinning. "And then" she continued, "I woke up, it was like 6:30 this morning, I never get up that early, but I couldn't get back to sleep." She stepped closer to Randy, "I'm scared Randy, what does it mean?"

He wrapped his arms around her, trying to understand, hoping to comfort her and himself, "I don't know, I don't know." Mary Anne said, "I have to go to the Ladies' room," then stepped back before walking to the hallway where the restrooms were located.

Looking down the line of people again, Randy saw the Palumbo family, Argento, Dominic, Vinnie and their mother and two sisters, all standing together, away from the line. He looked back to the anteroom and saw his mother still talking to Marie Bonavia, sister Terry and his father now standing at the casket, receiving their visitor's best empathy.

"Randy, we're really sorry about your brother," came over his shoulder. Turning left he saw Arlen Klaeckert and Dixie standing beside him, both wearing dark suits, ties, combed hair and shiny shoes. Surprised, he gasped slightly before extending his hand, "Thanks Mr. Klaeckert, thanks Dixie,"

Dixie clenched his hand tightly as he looked into Randy's eyes, "C'mere with me kid," and they stepped together, closer to the chairs, away from the soft din.

"You need to understand something *now*," Dixie began, his voice not loud but clear, "Your family is hurting really bad, all of them. Your parents can't begin to think, so you gotta step up and be a man."

Randy gulped, "Be a man? How? I'm only seventeen, well almost eighteen."

"It's not about age, someone has to be alert, watching, being sure they're safe. You'll get your time later, right now, they need someone they trust watching out for them."

"How do I do that?"

Dixie released his grip; Randy's hand was almost numb. "When you think about your brother, what do you remember?"

Randy thought about Michael playing baseball, combing his hair, how everyone liked him. How he talked about marrying Mary Anne, becoming a butcher in her grandfather's meat market. Remembering Michael's face, Randy smiled, "He was honest, he didn't cheat at anything. People liked him, he did what was right, even when others didn't like it."

"Uh-huh," Dixie nodded, "That's what people sometimes need, even when they don't know it. My brother was like that. He didn't care, was gonna do the right thing. That's what heroes do." Dixie looked around the area and then asked, "What was your brother thinking about his last day?"

Randy's mind went blank, he couldn't begin to imagine being on a helicopter just before it crashed, helplessly he mumbled, "I dunno,"

"Lemme tell you, he didn't think about himself, he was thinking about you, your brothers and sister, your parents. That's what heroes do; they think about all that's good. That gives them reason to do what nobody else would; do what's right, look out for everyone else."

Dixie's words entered Randy's chest, the idea of Michael thinking of his family from far away Viet Nam made sense.

"Randy," Dale called to his son, "Go out to the car and get that thermos laying under the front seat."

Randy nodded to his father and looked to Dixie, "Give me a minute Dix,"

As he walked out to the parking lot, Dixie's words echoed through his mind. Randy knew what the thermos was for, a special blend of Manhattan made to be added to ice in a styrofoam cup for his mother to sip. As he searched the Lincoln, Mary Anne started her return to the anteroom, only to be intercepted by Dominic Palumbo.

"Well, hello there," he smiled, "I heard angels came to these things, now I know it's true." Standing in the middle of the hallway, he watched her try to advance, stepping to her and blocking her path against the wall, "I'm Dominic. Who are you?"

"I'm Mary Anne," she replied, looking to the grand hallway, "can I get by please?"

"Mary Anne? Mary Anne who? Do I know you?"

"No. Michael Timmerman's my fiancé."

"*Was* your fiancé, I mean, he ain't doing so good now, you know?"

Mary Anne's nostrils flared as her cheeks flushed, anger surging through her eyes to his, "Let me by please."

"Hey, you going to the summer festival, down at Marsten Park? Why don't you go with me? I'll show you a good time, you know what I mean?"

"No thank you, now please, let me get by."

"What, you too good for me or something?"

"Hey asshole, she asked three times to get by; take the hint and step back."

Dominic wheeled around to see Dixie; his fists balled up, eyes locked forward.

"You, what's your problem man?"

"She told you she's not interested; leave her alone."

With Dominic's back turned, Mary Anne stepped to the other side of the narrow hallway and briskly skirted past the two, looking down, going to the anteroom to stand by her mother and Ruth.

"You little bastard," Dominic sneered, "you should mind your own business!"

"Or what?" Dixie asked, "You wanna do something? Go ahead." His body upright, fully prepared, Dixie stared at Dominic. As Randy walked to the anteroom with the thermos, he didn't see the two men in the hallway. Taking the thermos to his father, he then went to Mary Anne to find her shaking, her fingers trembling as she held the Kleenex to her nose.

"I have to go, are you going to Summer Fest next weekend?" Mary Anne asked.

Surprised, Randy gulped hard."I could, are you going?"

She nodded, "Im-hmm, would you go with me?"

Randy was astounded, never thinking a girl would ask him to take her anywhere, especially one as beautiful as Mary Anne Bonavia. He replied, "SURE, I mean, you want me to pick you up?"

Pete Bonavia walked up to them, Marie holding his arm, "Mary Anne honey, you ready?"

She turned to him, "One second Daddy," then looked back to Randy, "Saturday, say seven o'clock?"

"Yeah, Okay, I'll pick you up then."

As the Bonavia family walked to the evening light beyond the glass doors, Randy stood watching, wondering. A familiar voice asked him, "Hey kid, you alright?"

He looked to see Dixie standing to his right, hands in pockets, his face softer, now familiar, an old friend.Confident in the moment, Randy asked, "Dixie, you ever wonder if God does something for you, something you could never do on your own, just because he's God and he can do it?"

"Buddy, I pray for it. Like every time I pray into my cup."

"Pray? The white cup on the counter?"

"Every time somebody or something ticks me off, makes me sad, I say a prayer for the person or situation or whatever. I put that prayer in the cup and on Sunday, before Mass, I take my cup and sit in church, praying God will forgive me. Each time I want to remember Mom or my brother, I put prayers in that cup, hoping someday they'll help me."

******

The summer heat came in full force the first week of July, giving a sense of joy and relaxation for those seeking leisure and happiness. The days grew longer, the nights darker but warmer, enough so, the strongest memories of winter's cold, the long nights and cloudy days, all vanished in the temporary delight of the sun's daily warmth.

Michael Timmerman's funeral happened on such a sunny day, creating difficult feelings for survivors who so anxiously looked forward to seeing him once more. Now, no such reunion was possible. Randy Timmerman went to work and when not working the cash register, stocking paint cans, loading grass seed or fertilizer or helping Arlen and Dixie with something.

"Watch' a doing this weekend kid?" Dixie asked as they stacked garden hoses up besides the seed display.

"I'm taking Mary Anne to Summer Fest," Randy proclaimed proudly.

"That redheaded girl?"

"Yes sir," Randy stood up to his full height, wiping his brow, smiling broadly.

"Huh, go figure." Dixie kept his eyes level, "She desperate or something?"

"Screw you Dix," Randy quipped as they both broke into

laughter.

Dixie reached down and pulled up the last fifty-foot hose coil, dropping it on top of the others, "Come by the VFW stand, the first lemonade is on me."

******

Saturday couldn't arrive fast enough for Randy, each day of the week taking forever to complete. Thursday was payday and for the first time, Randy got to keep his entire earnings, the bill at Rollins Ford having been finally paid and Ruth's Lincoln just a beautiful as ever. Taking his money, Randy went to Bregner's Department Store and searched out the best fitting Levi's, plaid shirt and shoes for Saturday's date, telling Joey Walsh, "I got one shot to make Mary Anne notice me; I can't look like a doofus."

"You thinking she's going to date you?" Joey asked, half serious, half in jest.

"You think she won't," Randy stopped, his face wide considering the unthinkable.

131

"Uhm, man listen, she was expecting your brother to come home, just not in a box. She might be confused, you know, about how she feels and about who?" Joey stood still, watching his friend process the words.

Randy relaxed, his shoulders sloping a bit, "She asked me to take her man, I mean, why?"

"Look, I could be way off here," Joey saw Randy's confusion, "Just forget what I said."

"No, no, you're right, I gotta be cool." Randy looked at the clothes on the checkout counter, "And these are going to help."

******

Saturday was the warmest day yet, rising to ninety-five degrees by two o'clock and holding until five before starting to cool down. By seven o'clock, with sun descending to the west, the midwestern evening was a balmy eighty-two; a dream setting for teenagers attending a carnival-like event in a municipal park at river's edge. This would be a perfect Fourth of July, perfect weather, perfect date, a clear night sky for fireworks to dazzle everyone. Randy's good fortune continued when his mother allowed him to drive her Lincoln.

"You be careful young man," Dale charged.

"He will Dale," Ruth spoke evenly, "Won't you dear?"

"Yes Ma'am," Randy averred, looking directly to his mother, her smile soft and approving, her eyes still distant.

"Alright, you be home by midnight, you understand me?"

"Yes Ma'am,"

Taking the keys in hand, Randy strolled out to the garage and lifted the double door, hoping not to wrinkle his shirt or break a sweat from the strain. Turning the key, the robust engine fired up evenly as Randy pulled the gearshift and turned over the seat to view the rear as he backed down the driveway.

Cautiously, Randy travelled across town to Mary Anne's neighborhood, arriving at 6:55 P.M. After waiting a moment, he went to the front door and rang the doorbell. Standing on the small concrete stoop, he was surprised when Mary Anne opened the screen door and stepped out. She was a vision, her hair pulled back into a long, silky braid, almost reaching the middle of her back. She wore an off-white terry-cloth jumper that had gold buttons down the front and an attached belt with gold clasps. The short sleeves had tabs held up by gold buttons matching those on the side of each shorts-leg. Gold strap sandals complimented her small white purse with petite gold shoulder chain.

"W, w, wow," Randy stammered.

Mary Anne stopped, "What?"

"You, look beautiful." He blurted.

Instantly, Mary Anne blushed, "Oh, … you think?"

Randy nodded, gazing to her face, her hair, all of her, "Yes, yes I do."

"Well, thank you, I guess we should get going." She stepped down to the walk and after two paces stopped, "That's your car?"

"Yeah," Now Randy blushed, "No, it's my mom's, she's letting me drive it."

******

Taking extra caution, Randy parked the Lincoln at the far end of the parking lot, away from most cars, near a corner where a small building kept the tractor and other maintenance equipment. The couple walked to the festival entrance over three hundred feet away.

"Sorry about parking so far away," Randy said.

"It's okay, I'd be careful too."

"Well, I know that if anything happened; it would be expensive for me." Randy chuckled.

Mary Anne asked innocently, "What do you want to do, here at Summer Fest?"

Randy looked to the sun setting behind the bluff on the opposite side of the river, bright orange rays surging under light cirrus clouds and the blue evening. Putting his hands in his pockets, he shrugged, "I think I just want to have fun tonight, not worry or feel sad."

Mary Anne smiled, looking to the people lined up at the Ticket Booth, she agreed, "Me too."

They tried the usual rides; Randy shot free throws and won a small Teddy Bear which Mary Anne carried. As always, the food offerings were savory, sweet, hot and cold and almost everything except healthy. Looking to the VFW booth, Randy asked, "Want some lemonade?"

They proceeded to the stand where Dixie was waiting, "Well, look who's here! Want some lemonade?"

"Sure Dix, how's it going?"

"Busy, just like every year. How about you two? How's it

going for you?" He looked to Mary Anne, her eyes staring back, she kept silent. After an awkward moment Randy replied, "We're okay, having fun actually." He looked to Mary Anne, "Aren't we?"

Holding the small bear with both hands, she nodded, not saying a word.

"Let me get you those drinks," Dixie smiled and turned back to the serving counter.

"Randy, who is that man?" Mary Anne asked, her voice slightly more than a whisper.

"Him? That's Dixie, we work together at Klaeckert's"

"He's the man from my dream."

Randy's head jerked slightly, "What?"

"Here you go, two cold lemonades," Dixie proudly announced, his arms extended, a cup in each hand.

"Okay, wow, how much?"

"Told ya kid, these are on me." Dixie smiled bigger than Randy had ever seen him smile before. Dixie seemed transformed, there in the sunset, his face light, his smile broad, he was relaxed, enjoying himself.

"Okay, wow, well thanks Dixie!"

"Go have fun now, I'll see you two later." Dixie turned and went to the back of the stand, entering behind the dispenser and coming to stand behind the counter. Randy and Mary Anne turned and began walking back down the main walkway, quietly sipping their drinks. Something to his left caught Randy's eye, he paused mid-step to see the Palumbo brothers walking with three other boys, laughing, being loud. Quickly he turned to Mary Anne who was looking ahead to the gallery of rides, games and food vendors.

"You having fun?" He asked.

"What is that man's name?"

"Who?"

"Your friend, who gave us these drinks."

"You mean Dixie?"

"No, is his real name Brendan?"

Randy thought for a moment, remembering Arlen's story of Dixie, "Uhm, no, his name is Brian."

"You sure?" Mary Anne looked to Randy, serious, her eyes leveled directly to his. As Randy thought, Mary Anne continued, "I saw him in my dream last week, before Michael's visitation. He said his name was Brendan."

Really? You sure?" Randy was stalling, not sure how much to share. Mary Anne nodded, processing a moment before returning, "Yes, I've been thinking about my dream a lot. About how I heard Michael say he loved me and how peaceful it made me feel."

"Peaceful?"

They walked slowly as Mary Anne now spoke with confidence, her eyes open, certain, her voice full, "Hearing Michael say 'I love you' made it easier to accept him being gone."

"How's that?"

"I know Michael loved me. I know he's never coming back, here to me, he's gone forever. Not because he doesn't want me or doesn't care. He's gone, no pain, no sorrow. I always have his love."

The couple walked quietly, sipping their drinks, finally Randy asked, "So you're not sad anymore?"

"Sometimes, when I think about Michael, I'll feel a sadness. When someone you love dies, you can't help but carry that sadness. But you can't let it hold you, you can't die with that person."

They kept walking and watching other people, thinking to themselves about how death had changed them. Randy felt no longer on a date, but instead, acceptable in Mary Anne's presence, a way of being he thought easy for his brother but beyond him. Now, he saw himself more like Michael, an older brother, no longer a younger one. Feeling an urge to be open, he confessed, "Brian, you know Dixie? His older brother was Brendan."

Mary Anne stopped and let the disclosure hold her, her eyes showing her acceptance and understanding. After waiting a moment, she started walking again. Randy tried to recapture her attention, "Are you going to college Mary Anne?"

"I want to, are you?"

"I haven't really thought about it." Randy lied. He'd thought about college frequently. "But I'm not sure what I want to do, you know, once I graduate."

"I'm going away, somewhere, maybe out east." Mary Anne proclaimed.

"Oh yeah?" Dominic Palumbo boomed from behind them, "Where? New York? No, you look more like a Boston chick to me." His smile widened as he leaned over her shoulder, inserting his upper torso between Randy and she. Randy heard the snickering of Vinnie and the others behind him, he didn't look, he watched only Dominic leering at Mary Anne.

"So, this is how you are," Dominic continued, "I call you all week and you're here with him?"

Randy's eyes shot to Mary Anne's, she rolled her eyes and looked to Randy, "I never talked to him."

"Hey, don't talk to him" Dominic snapped, "I'm talking to you!"

"Go away," Mary Anne replied, "Get away from me."

"Yeah, beat it Dominic," Randy asserted.

"Hey!" Vinnie called, "Who you talking to?"

Randy looked behind to Vinnie standing behind, his shirt unbuttoned, showing his tee-shirt stretched over his ample waistline. He smiled, keeping one hand behind his back, tucked into his belted slacks. Randy had never seen the other three boys before. Dressed in Ban-Lon shirts and cuffed slacks, trying to look menacing some clenched their fists as they watched him.

Randy looked to Dominic, then the others,

"All of you, leave us alone."

"What if we don't, you gonna do something?" Dominic now turned his focus to Randy.

Nervous, feeling uncertain, Randy stood firm, extending his hand, "C'mon Mary Anne, let's go."

She took his hand and they stepped together, turning away, looking up to see two police officers in uniform, walking towards them and the Palumbo group. As they left Dominic threatened, "This ain't over."

Randy and Mary Anne kept walking, never looking back, sipping the last of their lemonades, unnerved by Dominic and Vinnie's presence. The evening had lost its glow and although it was only 10:30, both were ready to leave.

"You want to stay any longer?" Randy carefully asked.

"No, I mean, do you want to?" Mary Anne tried to sound enthusiastic but Randy saw her anxiety.

"I like being with you, talking with you, but,"

"We can go to my house, talk on the back porch if you like."

Now relaxed, Randy smiled, "Yeah, why don't we?"

They started walking to the parking lot, the lights and noise ebbing behind them. After twenty paces or so, Randy asked, "Mary Anne, do you ever feel like, I don't know, you're older and you don't want to be?"

"What?" Mary Anne looked to the grass ahead, walking slowly, thinking. Randy looked to the dark sky beyond the street lamps, where stars patiently twinkled in the night's deep, "Do you ever think things are changing around you, forcing you to grow up, before you're ready?"

After five or six steps she offered, "I've always been afraid I might not know enough." She looked to Randy, "And now, life's showing me how much I really don't know."

"Did you always want to go to college?"

"No. I thought I wanted to be married, have kids, live like my parents."

"Now you don't?"

Grimacing, she too looked to the stars, "I love my parents but;

I don't want their life."

Randy confessed to the night sky, "I watch my mom every day, she doesn't smile, doesn't talk. She makes dinner and smokes cigarettes, one after another. My dad doesn't talk much, he just sits out on the patio every night, smoking, drinking beer. If that's what being grown-up is; I gotta do something else."

"Like what?" Mary Anne looked to Randy intently, weaving her fingers together.

"I don't know, but I don't think staying here is my future. I'll be eighteen Wednesday; I have my senior year ahead. I have to register for the draft; I can't vote in an election but I can die for my country. I feel like all these adult things are crashing down on me."

Walking in silence the couple stayed close, not touching but connected, feeling the weight of each other's questions. Randy pulled the car keys out and began to unlock the passenger side door for Mary Anne when he heard steps in the gravel behind the maintenance building. He looked to his right to see Dominic Palumbo coming towards them.

"Yeah, thought you'd run home, you little pussy!" Dominic sneered as he took his right fist back. Before he could throw his punch, Randy bolted at him, tackling him at the diaphragm, knocking him down to the ground so hard, the air in Dominic's lungs rushed out, leaving him gasping and gulping and wriggling on the grass like a landed fish.

Randy rolled back and looked to see Vinnie and the others standing around Mary Anne, one boy, a blond boy with pale skin, thin and wiry, grabbing at Mary Anne's arms saying, "C'mon baby, let's get out of here." She slapped his face with a full, broad palm, snapping his head sharply left.

Randy jumped to his feet and ran to help her, not seeing Vinnie reach behind his back. As Randy got even with Vinnie, Vinnie swung and the overhead light gleamed off the surface of something in Vinnie's right hand, coming down on Randy's left ear.

"Whad'ya think you're doing punk!" Vinnie yelled as he struck Randy hard. The impact made a loud crunch sound, striking the side of Randy's head and somehow cutting him at the temple. The sudden blow's force knocked Randy to the ground face down, giving Vinnie opportunity to drop his two-hundred plus pound body on the small of Randy's back. Others came forward and began kicking Randy's ribs, saying things Randy couldn't understand; his hands covering his ears. His left hand felt blood trickling on his cheek as his ribs felt the toes of Cuban-heeled shoes.

Dominic had recovered enough to come to Mary Anne and as he grabbed her wrist he ordered, "Take care of the lightweight fellas, I've got a date."

"RRAAANNNDDDYYY!!" Mary Anne screamed.

Looking up to his right, he saw Dominic wrenching Mary Anne's arm, dragging her with him. He sneered as they walked toward the back of the maintenance building, "C'mon baby, you're going with me."

As the stark light and shadows showed the crime, Randy felt rage exploding in his chest. Though his head was throbbing, his mind cleared, focusing on Mary Anne. Putting his hands palms down on the ground, he pressed himself up, lifting Vinnie with him as the others froze in place. As Vinnie rolled off backwards, Randy stood and faced the blond pompadour boy who now had a pocket switchblade in his hand.

"C'mon pussy, you wanna try something?!" He lunged at Randy, knifepoint first, aiming at Randy's chest. Instinctively, like boxing with brother Michael, Randy, the only left-handed child in his family, swatted the knife-hand down as his right cross landed flush on the boy's jaw. Randy's punch was so powerful, the skinny boy went to the ground, his abdomen falling on his right hand and the knife.

"OOHHH GGOODDD," The boy cried, then rolled over on his back, displaying the knife buried to the hilt in his stomach. "Holy shit, holy shit!" one of the others hissed before pushing his cohort's arm, "Let's get outta here!" Immediately, both turned and ran towards the festival lights.

Randy looked next to where he thought Vinnie would be, only

to see empty space. He started running to the maintenance shed, going the same route he saw Dominic take Mary Anne. Rounding the building's corner, the blue-white incandescent light showed four persons; Dominic holding Mary Anne with one hand, Dixie holding Dominic's other hand, his right hand, his strongest hand. Mary Anne gripped Dominic's hand with both of hers and Vinnie, standing in the light with both hands pointing a silver gun. All four people were frozen still and looked to Randy who brought his sprint to an abrupt halt.

"Get back Randy!" Vinnie yelled, now turning the gun on him. He was shaking, "Get back I tell ya, or I'll, …"

Seizing the moment, keeping his fabled gunner's-grip on Dominic's wrist, Dixie commenced punching with his free hand; his mallet-like fist hammering Dominic's cheek, jaw and nose, once, twice, three times, four.

Mary Anne fought harder to shake free, bending over to bite Dominic's fingers and knuckles. Dixie's punches returned time and again, like a metal-stamping machine knocking out pieces, 'whack-whack-whack-whack.' Dominic's face quickly became a blood-flesh pulp and as he sank to his knees he let go of Mary Anne. Dixie paused a moment, breathing heavily, still holding Dominic's right wrist. Seeing his brother reduced to a pile, Vinnie turned back, yelling, "You son-of-a-bitch!!"

A telltale 'CRACK' broke the night air, then, 'CRACK,

CRACK' and Mary Anne screamed. Randy watched Dominic collapse; then Dixie went down too.

"OH MY GOD! OH MY GOD!!" Vinnie pleaded as he ran quickly to his brother, lying on the grass under the pole light, "Dominic! Get up, get up!"

Mary Anne got to Dixie first and lifted his head off the ground. Randy slid to his knees opposite Mary Anne, Dixie's cream-colored shirt with large light blue crosshatches now showing two large, dark crimson stains, one in his abdomen, one between the second and third buttons. He was gasping, gulping, his lips moving as his eyes searched the blue-white haze above.

"Dix; Dix, you're gonna be alright, I'm right here!" Randy proclaimed despite his mind being completely empty. Randy took Dixie's right hand and interlocked it with his at the thumbs. Two police officers came running up, "What's going on?!" one demanded.

"He's been shot!" Mary Anne yelled.

"Shot!? By who?"

Randy looked back to see Vinnie, kneeling over Dominic, crying, "I'm sorry, Dom, I'm sorry." The silver pistol lay on the ground and Randy noticed a small hole, a similar crimson corona over the hole in Dominic's lemon-yellow shirt, now looking white under the incandescent light. Vinnie bent closer to Dominic, "What,

I can't hear you?"

Seeing Dominic's now mashed profile, Randy thought no matter how well he healed, Dominic would never look the same. The moment was pierced by the only words from Dominic Randy clearly heard; "I can't feel my legs."

Trying to grasp Dominic's meaning, Randy felt Dixie's hand squeeze his. He turned to his friend laying in the crisp blue-white light, lips moving but no sound. Bending his ear to Dixie's lips, he listened intently. Dixie whispered, "Be a man, kid. Be a man now."

Randy felt his tears growing and couldn't stop them. He looked to Dixie who now looked whiter, his eyes open, searching above the artificial light. Holding his other hand gently, Mary Anne leaned forward to Dixie's face, "Brian, I saw Brendan the other night, he said it's okay."

Dixie's eyes widened, he tried lifting his head to look directly at Mary Anne, "You saw Brendan?" he asked. Mary Anne nodded, letting a slight smile come forth. Dixie looked back to the heavens, smiling ever so slightly. Taking a deep breath, he spoke, "Hey Bren," his eyes glistened, shining, his countenance brighter. Breathing more deeply, he nodded, "Yeah, they're good kids."

Dixie's eyes darted towards Randy, then centered and his smile grew larger, as he exhaled one last time out came, "Ma."

A police officer knelt down, "Okay, whatta we got here?"

Mary Anne and Randy's tears were the only response. The officer pushed his hat back and called to his partner, "Mel, we need the coroner's office, got one for the morgue."

******

It was almost three o'clock in the morning when Randy pulled the Lincoln into the family garage. A police squad car rolled to a stop in the street, at the driveway's edge. Dale Timmerman got up from his patio seat and walked to the garage door, meeting Randy as he came out. "Good evening, Mister Timmerman," the approaching officer softly spoke. Dale told Randy, "Wait for me on the patio."

They stood in the breezeway almost twenty minutes as the officer recounted the evening's events with Dale occasionally nodding, asking questions. Randy wanted to listen, though he really didn't care what was said; he was there, he knew what happened. Everybody else can go to hell.

Randy stopped thinking long enough to hear the officer say,

"He's a real good kid, stood up for the girl, stayed with his friend till the end. I'm not his father, but I'd go easy on him, he's had a pretty rough night."

"Thank you, officer." Dale nodded, the orange glow of his cigarette bobbing up and down in the dark. As the sound of the squad car driving away diminished, Dale came back to the patio, the soft glow of the yellow insect-repelling bulb casting a strange glow on the wrought iron table and chairs, a large metal cooler sat next to one chair, a large ashtray holding numerous remains and ash on the table. Dale returned to his chair; his beer now warm as the night. Gulping down its last portion, he crushed the can with one hand; plumbers can grip things too.

"So, how you doing son?" Dale lifted the stainless-steel lid and reached into the cooler, pulling out another Budweiser. Randy sat, letting his brain line up random thoughts, trying to assemble a simple reply. He leaned back in the chair next to Dale's, the cooler between them.

"In the last six weeks, my brother, who I knew all my life, was killed and I'll never see him again. My friend, who I just met this summer, died tonight trying to help me and I'll never see him again either. I'm turning eighteen next week and I feel old, like I'm not a kid anymore, but I don't think I'm grown up. I feel like the longer I live, the more I have to try to survive. I never thought about life or death before; I just wanted to drink beer and get laid. Now, I think there's way too much that could go wrong any moment and there's not much I can do about it. It doesn't seem fair but; I don't know what else life could be."

The two men sat in yellow-washed silence, looking beyond the table's edge to the darkness.Randy asked his father, "Why are you out here so late?"

"Well," Dale shifted in his seat, "I kinda fucked up."

"What?"

"Today's your mother's and my wedding anniversary. I completely forgot and didn't get her a card or anything."

"Sounds to me like a screw-up more than a fuck-up." Randy opined. Dale looked to his son, the shadows covering his wrinkled brow, "What the hell you talking about?"

Randy looked to his father, letting a wry smile emerge in the yellow light, "A screw-up you can fix; a fuck-up you can't do nothing about."

After a minute, Dale lifted the cooler lid and pulled another Budweiser out, cold water dripping off his hand. Extending his arm, he gave his son the beer. The two looked to each other and nodded solemnly; drinking in silence until sunrise.

Mothers and Millstones

The morning sun shone brightly on the school's east parking lot, illuminating Spring semester's last full week. Wednesday, May 24th, 1961, started with the customary quiet, even paced actions of St. Philomena's Elementary staff. Behind the church, children gathered in the playground before lining up by classes at precisely 8:25 A.M. Each grade proceeded past the brilliant white marble statue of The Blessed Virgin, through two doors and into the ell-shaped building.

The morning breeze was light, laughter and squeals flowed over grass and asphalt and clouds occasionally drifted through the bright blue. Six more school days before summer recess would only be limited by doctor's appointments, summer camps, vacations and eventually, tedium from playing all day.

Eunice Daugherty pulled her Biscayne sedan into the church parking space, turning off the engine as she commanded her three children, "Michael, be sure your brother and sister get in line on time, okay?" The taller boy seated in back, rolled his eyes, nodding obediently.

"Mark James, I don't want to hear about any class disruptions, do you understand me?" Her emerald green eyes searched the rearview mirror, finally focusing on the shorter, auburn-haired lad slouched behind his mother. He too rolled his eyes, but out to the blue sky, "Yeyass, Ma'am."

Eunice looked to little Mary Rose, nestled between her brothers, a cherubic colleen of ebony curls, blazing green eyes and freckles that danced ever so lightly across her peach-colored cheeks. The mother's green eyes smiled to the daughter's as they shared affection through the reflected view.

"You be a good girl, Mary Rose, okay?"

"Momma I don't want to play; can I sit in the office with you?"

"Not today, honey. Sister Carmella wouldn't approve."

The little pout charmed Eunice, causing her to smile as she opened the car door. Her children flowed out the rear doors before the boys rolled the windows partially down in anticipation of the days' heat. As her children ran to the playground, Eunice headed to the school office.

Stepping quickly up three cement stairs, she turned right into the lobby and entered the Principal's Office; the sentry post and general information station. Eunice's desk waited, a simple dulled olive-green metal with composite top holding a telephone, calendar desk mat, upright file holder, Michael's Cub Scout pencil can, a single bulb lamp and two note pads, all ready for deployment.

Eunice went to the supply closet where an upright West Bend

coffee pot signaled a fresh brew ready. Pouring a cup, she returned to her desk and as she sat, her telephone clarioned the day's first issue, ringing and flashing a white light under the first button on the dial face. Sister Carmella Rose, a tall, regal looking nun, turned into the office as Eunice picked up the phone's receiver and pressed the flashing button down.

"Good morning, St. Philomena's Elementary School. How may I help you?" rolled out like so many times before. Sister Carmella Rose, in her Order of St. Dominic white habit and black headdress smiled to Eunice while gliding silently to her office.

"This is Patricia Keagan," The voice offered.

"Patricia, good morning, it's Eunice."

"Oh, hi, my son, Paulie Keagan, won't be in school today."

"Oh? Is he sick?"

"No, he's dead."

The words punched Eunice and she gasped loudly, stunned, her mind suddenly compressed under a single stupefying moment, "I'm sorry, what'd you say?"

"He hung himself last night. My son is dead."

The telephone's hang up click led to a silence holding Eunice, struggling to comprehend. She sat motionless, trying to reassemble mentally. After three or four minutes, Eunice slowly stood up and cautiously walked to Sister Carmella's office. The daily announcements by either Sister Carmella or Eunice were due in ten minutes. But Eunice wasn't sure what to think, or say, or suggest about this most alarming news. Stepping to the doorjamb's edge, Eunice softly asked, "Sister, can I tell you something?"

The stately nun was seated and looked to Eunice with her pleasant smile, "Good morning Mrs. Daugherty, please come in." Eunice walked steadily to the chair, a plain, partan design of blond wood, probably oak, green vinyl padding on the seat, arms and back, before Sister's desk. Sitting down, Eunice kept her torso forward, her fingers tightly interlaced.

"I just got a call from Patricia, I mean, Mrs. Keagan. She said Paulie Junior's dead." Her voice was flat, simply reporting facts while Eunice's body trembled, her eyes searching the nun's face, seeking understanding. Sister Carmella blanched, her face immediately matching her habit's whiteness. She brought her hands together, fingers aligned as if to pray.

"Dead? Was there an accident?"

"No. She said he hung himself."

The nun gasped aloud, her head jerking back, eyes wide. "Hung himself? Oh, dear God!"

Eunice searched her mind, unable to fathom suicide by a ten-year old boy. Nodding slowly, Eunice felt tears building as her breathing shortened, her body shivering, "I can't believe it. I know the Keagan's."

Sister Carmella Rose sat back, bringing her fingers to her lips, still ready to pray. The silence was broken by Sister Carmella's telephone, jingling loudly, another flashing white light.

"Good morning, this is Sister Carmella Rose," the nun calmly offered the receiver mouth-piece, her eyes falling to her desktop. Suddenly, she looked up, out her window across the drive to the south, to the rectory.

"Yes," she looked back to Eunice, "Yes Father, I just learned myself." Taking a ball-point pen in hand, Sister Carmella started jotting down words on her notepad. "I see, yes," her head nodding to the instructions entering her ear, "I understand."

She leaned back, holding the receiver in her left hand as she motioned with her right to Eunice, whispering, "Who's class is Paulie Keagan in?"

Automatically, Eunice responded, "Sister Dominic James'"

Hearing that answer, Sister Carmella's face sagged before replying, "Yes Father, I will." Hanging up the telephone, she sat back in her chair, her eyes dancing left and right, pen hand shaking. Inhaling deeply, Sister Carmella pressed back into her stately poise, "That was Father O'Neill. He's been informed of Paulie Keagan's passing. Father Devine is with the family now."

Eunice exhaled, sagging into her chair. Looking to her hands, her tension was confirmed by her fingers' white numbness. After three deep, slow breaths, she asked, "What should we tell the class?"

"We're to say nothing right now. Father O'Neill will confer with Father Devine and the staff will be informed later today. Please notify all the teachers we'll be meeting today at 4:30."

Eunice accepted the sister's directive, but wondered why the class wouldn't be told. These were new times for Catholics.

John Fitzgerald Kennedy had been elected president, taking office a mere four months ago. After all the scrutiny raised during the presidential campaign, many parishes' wanted life to continue peaceably, without tension or discomfort. Being Catholic had become acceptable; being Irish-American Catholic was in vogue.

******

By 10:30, the day was progressing at its customary pace. Still amazed at Patricia Keegan's voice, so flat, mechanical, Eunice wanted to put her thoughts and feelings in order. She called the rectory office hoping her resource was available. The phone rang only twice before a woman politely answered, "St. Philomena's Parish Rectory, this is Madeline, how may I help you?"

"Oh good, you're there."

"High, how's it going?"

"Didn't you hear?"

"Yeah, I asked without thinking," Madeline's blush warmed Eunice's composure. "I'm sure you've got a lot more happening than I do."

"Not really,"

"No? What's going on?"

"Nothing, everybody's acting like it's another Wednesday."

"Really?"

"What's the word over there?"

"Uhm, I can't talk now, but we've been busy this morning." Madeline coughed into her free hand, "Want to meet for lunch?"

"Can we? I was hoping we could." Eunice's relief gushed to Madeline's ear.

"Sure, the orchard picnic table, say noon?"

"I'll be there" Eunice confirmed.

"Okay, bye." Madeline hung up and Eunice felt relieved,

looking at the clock above the office doorway; eighty-five minutes until a chance to breathe.

Madeline Costello was a young woman the others at St. Philomena's either admired or completely distrusted. The third of seven children, Madeline decided before high school graduation, marriage and children were not in her near future. Working for two years at her local drug store, Madeline saved money before applying to Flight Stewardess school in Ft. Lauderdale, Florida.

Sixteen months later she began flights between Chicago and the east coast. Three years later, she routinely travelled to Europe, all over America and occasionally to Japan. Madeline made good on her promise to herself not to live her mother's life.

Now, thirty-four years old, married to Tom, they live comfortably, but they are sometimes the subjects of rumors or envy; they have no children. One rumor suggests due to Madeline's promiscuity as a stewardess; she has been damaged, unable to conceive. Another suggests Tom married Madeline to cover his true sexual preferences. Neither slur has any truth; Madeline was sexually abused as a child and Tom likes to wear Italian loafers to work and Sunday Mass.

Precisely at noon, Eunice took her modest lunch out to the last rows of the apple orchard, three-hundred feet or so east of the school and rectory. The orchard was planted by the farmer who sold the property to the Archdiocese in 1946, against the wishes of many local residents.

A sturdy picnic table made of wide, rough planks remained under a taller tree. There, under the shade, in a light breeze, Eunice and Madeline occasionally enjoyed lunch, gossip, fashion magazines and friendship without fear of bearing overheard.

"So," Madeline started, "Busy morning, I'll bet."

Eunice looked out to the street, taking her sandwich from its waxed paper wrapper, "No, well, at first, but pretty quiet after that."

Taking out some celery sticks and carrots, Madeline peeled the clear plastic wrap with deliberate patience. Eunice watched Madeline deftly wrap a bologna slice around her carrot stick before taking a bite.

"Where'd you learn to eat that?"

"Old stewardess trick." Madeline replied, keeping her lip pressed while crunching softly, "Gotta keep the weight off you know."

A moment later, Madeline swallowed before reaching into her lunch bag and retrieving her daily bottle of Coca-Cola. Taking a bottle opener from her purse, she plucked the cap off. A quick swig preceded her announcement, "Well, there's a lot going on by me."

"Really? Like what?"

"Another problem with Sister Dominant James" Madeline

smirked as she brought a celery stick to her teeth.

"Another?"

Nodding while chewing, Madeline's face lost its impish grin. Guiding her hair back off her face as the breeze pushed by, she looked to the buildings, "There's been complaints this year, two, no, three I think."

"What's the problem?" Eunice innocently asked.

"I don't know exactly, but O'Neill has been on the phone to the archdiocese this morning again. They can't find anywhere for her to go."

"Go?" Eunice bit into her chicken-salad sandwich, waiting.

"She's been a nun for over forty years, but never been at any parish longer than three." Madeline looked directly to Eunice as another bologna-carrot bite followed. After a moment, Madeline confided, "And she's been at a lot of parishes, believe me."

"Is that a problem, I mean," Eunice stopped to think before reframing her question, "What does that mean, if she's frequently changing parishes?"

Though younger, in many ways Madeline was more worldly, knowledgeable than most women. Thinking while she chewed her lunch, she sat at the table recalling her time flying. Swallowing her food, she looked to the sky, "I flew for almost nine years and I worked with about ten different crews. That was the usual way, because of where the crews were flying to. I asked to be stateside at first, so I stayed with one of two crews and I worked regularly. When I wanted to go to Europe, I requested being assigned to an international crew. I worked with three different crews for three years, but just those three."

Listening intently, Eunice still felt confused, "Did Sister Dominic asked to be assigned here?"

"Near as I can tell, she never asked to be anywhere. She took her vows in Baltimore, was assigned later to St. Louis, then Boston, then Cleveland I think, and then," another swig of Coca-Cola cleared her throat, "Minneapolis, Chicago, I can't remember, but she's never been anywhere longer than three years, I know that."

"Maybe she's sent where she's needed." Eunice couldn't comprehend a nun being a problem. Nuns were kind, loving, taking vows of chastity, poverty and service. Eunice thought of her school years, the nuns she confided in, women dedicated to service and children's welfare, it seemed inconceivable a nun could be undesirable. Eunice continued, "How do you know she wasn't requested by those parishes? Maybe she's really good at something they needed?"

Madeline stopped her eating, her hand almost dropping her apple, her face taking a cynical mask, like the older sister disbelieving the younger's naiveté, "When a parish requests someone, the make it through the archdiocese. Dominant James' record simply says, '*Transferred to*'; nobody asked for her."

Eunice finished her sandwich, neatly folding up her waxed paper before taking an orange out of her bag. Piercing the orange's hide with her thumbnail, she waited, knowing Madeline had more to say.

"Do you remember Sister Bernadette, the shorter, kinda round nun, with the mustache?" Madeline's face broke into a laugh as she tried to keep chewed apple bits in place. Covering her mouth with her hand, her body shook, tremors erupting from within. Eunice also laughed, placing the orange on the table, she turned her head aside, "Yes, but I," her laughter overtook her, "I never thought anyone else noticed her mustache!" she guffawed, closing her eyes, letting her body shake.

Gasping to compose herself, Madeline held her fingers to her lips, her eyes glassy, her apple patiently waiting on the table. "Ohh, aww, okay, well she was transferred to Madison. Apparently, she was a holy terror about assigning kitchen or housekeeping duties and nobody could get along with her, so, they sent her to Madison.

Things like that happen all the time. People forget nuns and priests are just humans doing a different job. Just like pilots, there's good ones and not so good ones. People think because they're wearing a certain uniform, they don't make mistakes. Believe me, they're no different from you or me."

Eunice considered Madeline's words, "Yes, but this time, a child has died. Certainly nothing like that has ever happened before, has it?"

Madeline's smile melted under the tree's shade, her face becoming somber, emotionless, "Not here, not until today, nobody's ever died."

Madeline's words hung in the air while Eunice examined them, mentally reviewing the phrases like artwork hanging on a wall. New imagery began surfacing, "Someone's been hurt before?"

Madeline's eyes looked directly to Eunice, focused, serious. A slight nod came next, her chewing now indiscernible. Eunice took an orange wedge and softly bit into it, trying to understand the weight of Madeline's silence. Finishing her food, Madeline began collecting her lunch bag and bottle, "Families threatened legal action, went to the attorney, Mr. Gilbert."

"Here? Families? More than one?" The thought overwhelmed Eunice.

"I've said enough; I need to get back." Madeline stood up from the table, straightened her skirt and while trying to straighten her hair, offered to the open air, "All I know is this; I'm a Catholic and if I had any children, they wouldn't be in a catholic school."

Between 3:30 and 3:35, one by one, Eunice rounded up her children, marching them directly to the waiting Chevy. "Michael, you watch your brother and sister until I get home tonight."

As she opened the car door, she looked to see his reluctant nod. Mark James pulled open the other rear door and waited for Mary Rose to slide across the sticky vinyl back seat. The engine came to life, Eunice quickly checked the vehicle's perimeter, pulling the gearshift lever into position. Once in her driveway, she parked the car and twisted across the driver seat-back to proclaim final instructions.

"Remember, change your clothes, do your homework then you can go to the park, but only together. I should be home by six o'clock, so dinner will be a little late tonight, okay?" She looked to her three children lined up, faces blank, waiting to escape. They all nodded, then the boys pulled the door latches and jumped out, fleeing to the side door of the small suburban home. Mary Rose sat looking to her mother, her eyes searching. Eunice asked, 'What is it honey?'

The child looked ahead through the windshield, peering

forward but not seeing. After a moment Mary Rose looked to Eunice, "Oh, nothing." She lifted her two books and started sliding toward the door Mark James left open. Two short slides and she was outside, heading to the house door also left open by her brother. Walking slowly, deep in thought, Mary Rose stopped for a moment before looking to Eunice waiting behind the steering wheel. Their eyes met and Eunice knew her daughter was distressed. Charged with an urge to get out of the car and scoop Mary Rose up in her arms, Eunice gripped the steering wheel, resisting a holistic force.

"I need to get back," she announced, then yanked the metal gearshift lever down. Turning herself over the seat to look out the rear window, she kept her focus backward, never seeing Mary Rose enter the house. Driving to St. Philomena's, Eunice fought anxious moments, smothered in shame.

******

St. Philomena's was a simple one-story ell-shaped brick building, having sixteen classrooms, a main office and an open area that doubled as the cafeteria and parish hall. The space was rumored to be for future classrooms, but despite the burgeoning enrollment, children still ate their lunches in shifts and parishioners routinely held monthly meetings.

Eunice retrieved the steno pad from her desk and hurried down the north hall to the cafeteria. She walked into the open space towards the six east-west rows, each having four rectangular tables complimented by beige-colored metal folding chairs. Nuns and lay teachers waited, quietly chatting, some with notepads before them on the table. Eunice walked to the far eastern corner of the row identified as '#1' by a plastic card taped to the table top.

Eunice looked to the eleven nuns and four lay teachers, all female, some of who smiled and nodded. The atmosphere was late afternoon heat, milder Midwestern humidity with tension floating just beneath. As Eunice sat, Father O'Neill appeared, coming from the hallway towards the tables. Behind him, walking with their heads bowed down, Sister Carmella Rose and Sister Dominic James. A step behind Sister Carmella Rose, Sister Dominic clasped her hands together, two pens coming up as her left forearm pressed a legal pad to her chest. Sister Dominic James, a larger, older woman, her face pale, walked slowly, her back slightly hunched. She resembled a white missile warhead in rimless spectacles.

Walking to the end of Table #1, Father O'Neill waited as Sister Carmella came to the seat immediately to his right, between he and Eunice. Sister Dominic walked to the end of Table #2, taking the seat closest to Table #1, behind Sister Beatrice, blocked from Sister Carmella Rose's view. After clearing his throat, Father O'Neill began, "In the name of the father, son and holy ghost."

In unison, everyone made the sign of the cross with him, some bowing their heads, some closing their eyes. Father O'Neill opined, "Gracious heavenly father, we come before you in prayer, asking your grace upon us at this most difficult time. Look not on our sins, but instead deliver us for your glory, in Jesus' name we pray."

"Amen" everyone dutifully replied, some fully, some whispering, some then making the sign of the cross again.

Looking to the faces lining the table before him, Father O'Neill began a somber and serious message, "Sisters, ladies, I've called you together to share some difficult news. We've lost one of our students to the evil one once more."

Some heads jerked back slightly as audible gasps went up, some eyes searched the other faces, but nothing was said.

"Paul Keagan Junior was taken from us during the night. He was a student in Sister Dominic James' class." Father O'Neill paused, tilting his head slightly to his left, toward Sister Dominic James.

"I'm sure in the next few days, this terrible news will come to our students. I want to be certain we can address any concerns. I sent Father Devine to the family home when I first heard this morning. He's returned and advised me the family is doing as well as can be expected."

Sister Carmella looked down the table to detect questions or doubts, checking staff expressions. Completing her sweep, she looked across the table over Beatrice's shoulder. Sister Dominic sat sideways to Table #2, her back to the others, facing Father O'Neill, writing notes on her legal pad. Eunice also took notes in shorthand for transcription into school records. Keeping her head down, she listened for the next voice, ready to record whatever was said. After a ten second silence, Father O'Neill asked "Has anybody encountered any questions about this?"

Without looking up, Eunice sensed discomfort winding around her table. Some throats cleared, quiet swallows as hands were clasped on the table or in laps, eyes furtively looked anywhere but to the priest. At last, Sister Patrice, an eighth-grade teacher seated approximately fifteen feet from Father O'Neill, courageously spoke, "Father, I heard some boys in my class talking this afternoon."

Eunice looked to the nun; *some boys* could include her Michael. Looking back to her pad, Eunice focused her eyes down and her ears downwind, waiting to detect every syllable uttered. Sister Patrice continued, "The Buscemi boys went to their dentist this morning. Their father, the Fire Department Assistant Chief, brought them back to school. Well, apparently, he was called to the Keagan house. The boys reported Paulie Keagan Junior, was hanged or hanged himself. Is that true?"

More murmuring, shuffling of feet under the table, shifting in metal folding chairs or looking away; only Sister Beatrice openly expressed surprise. Father O'Neill held his position, arms extended on the table, fingers interlaced, his face never changing. After a moment, he calmly reported, "Yes sister, I'm afraid Satan convinced this poor child to end his life."

Another, softer wave of distress washed across all the women, except one; Sister Dominic kept writing, her hand etching into the pad while the others processed this news. Sensing the need to establish calm, Father O'Neill spoke, focusing on the four lay teachers, "Ladies, we must maintain professional composure. Rumors or gossip can be very harmful to St. Philomena's and yourselves as well."

"Father, I don't understand," Mrs. Delores Roberts, a sixth-grade teacher began, "a student is hanged in their home, and we must be professional? What does that mean?"

"His closet," Sister Patrice interjected, "the boys said he hung himself."

A collective gasp, louder than before, rushed off the tables up to the acoustic tiled ceiling, some mouths dropped open, the shock wave lifting their eyes to one another first, then to the priest. Father O'Neill knew he had to suppress this nervous spirit.

"Sisters, ladies, let's remain calm!" His normally taciturn face turning red at the cheeks, "We must keep our eyes on the bigger picture here."A hush fell over the tables as quickly as the unrest erupted."We cannot let rumors, or misinformation discredit all St. Philomena's is to this parish, the diocese and Roman Catholic church. We all saw how the world attacked President Kennedy for his faith. There are many out there, looking, waiting for any opportunity to attack us."

Some eyebrows wrinkled as minds worked to digest Father O'Neill's statement. But before anyone dared respond or question, he continued, "We must have a positive image, we must keep our enrollment growing, we must continue our education revenue to help pay the diocese debt for our building. Our parish isn't the most affluent, we have some faithful families who tithe regularly, but that isn't nearly enough."

"Father," Mrs. Mary Thanikos, a seventh-grade teacher spoke next. A shorter, raven-haired woman, curvaceous, fond of high heels and red lipstick, she smiled and laughed frequently, freely. Her sparkle and warmth irritated some nuns, who occasionally complained to Sister Carmella. Mrs. Thanikos accepted students unconditionally; in return they respected her. Looking quickly about the tables, she looked to Father O'Neill, "We have what, three-hundred and sixty students here?"

"Three-hundred and eighty-two" Sister Carmella replied.

"Three hundred and eighty-two students and sixteen teachers. We have classrooms filled to their limit. Was there any indication of trouble with this student? Did anyone see or hear anything troubling? Whose class was he in?"

Father O'Neill and Sister Carmella stiffened, Sister Dominic stopped her writing, her face set, she turned to face Mrs. Thanikos. Before Father O'Neill could respond, Sister Dominic, in firm voice, addressed the room. "Paul Keagan was a fourth-grader in my class. I have a split class; fourteen fifth-grade and sixteen fourth-grade students. He was a poor, mediocre student, given unfortunately, to daydreaming, laziness and occasional belligerence. I tried my best to educate the child but, he lacked discipline, possibly he came from a difficult home."

"Lacked discipline?" Mrs. Roberts voice bordered on indignant, "What fourth-grader doesn't lack discipline? Does this have anything to do with Monday?"

Sister Dominic's eyes narrowed to the middle-aged woman sitting diagonally across the tables from her, "What do you mean?"

Delores Roberts was a tall, solid, German-American Catholic woman, tough as an Army drill sergeant. An educator for over twenty years, she now taught sixth-grade; rarely misspoke and even more rarely ever blinked. Folding her arms in front of her, she leaned on the table, speaking louder to be sure everyone heard her.

"I was leaving the school, around four forty-five and as I passed your classroom door sister, I heard some crying. I went in and there, by the blackboard, in the corner by your supply closet, was Paulie Keagan, head on his desk, crying his eyes out. I asked him why was he still here? And why was he crying? He looked around the room, then to me, his face puffy and red like a strawberry, gulping and sobbing, choking on tears, he shook his head and said 'I don't know."

A tear forming in Mrs. Roberts right eye, she pushed on, "I asked him why are you up here? What did you do? Again, he shook his head and started crying again, coughing, choking. He cried, 'Sister said I need to pray, to Jesus, to ask him to forgive me!' I said, 'What did you do?' And the boy, that poor, precious little boy, kept saying, 'I don't know, I don't know."

Tears now flowed down many faces, including Eunice's. She searched valiantly for the single tissue she kept in the left pocket of her dress, groping while writing, tears hanging on her chin.

Mrs. Roberts took a deep breath, looked to the other women seated at the table before returning her glare directly to Sister Dominic, "I wonder sister, in all my years of education, I've never seen a child so crushed, so despairing, giving up all dignity in pain and sorrow. I wonder, what could a child, any child, _that_ child, possibly have done to deserve being isolated like that?"

Eunice looked up to Sister Dominic's red face, her eyes angry, her lips pressed firmly together. The room shrank to the tables' immediate area as the air grew heavy, a current of disgust, fueled by anger, disbelief and horror swirled through minds and hearts at table #1.

Sister Dominic resumed her defense, "Everyday I've got thirty children in my class, some diligent students; most well-behaved. Paulie Keagan was neither. I was never trained to educate such children; I'm an administrator. Paulie Keagan was disruptive, rarely prepared for class. For the good of the fourth and fifth grade students, I had to separate him as he tended to impair their lessons. He was a poor student; possibly mentally defective."

Mrs. Thanikos exploded, her face approaching her lipstick's red, her body trembling, "In all my years, here and in Chicago, I've never heard such a heartless excuse! I can't imagine what any ten-year-old boy could do to deserve such terrible treatment!"

Eunice also felt angry, emotional lava surging from within. Being Patricia Keagan's friend, she knew of the family's struggles over the last three years. She knew of two still-births Patricia suffered in the seven years between Paulie's birth and three-year-old Patricia Marie. Gamely, Eunice slowed her mind, stifling her emotions, she had to record this meeting accurately. The time for her feelings would be later.

"Sisters, ladies," Father O'Neill tried recapturing control, "If we hope to remain solvent, which includes education salaries, we cannot lose more families from the parish. Every monthly diocese meeting, I have to listen to Father Augustine's boasting about Our Lady of Peace's growing enrollments, improving revenue, their need to buy more books. That new subdivision, Hawthorne something, going up in his area, another one hundred and sixty-five houses. If we cannot demonstrate the ability to deliver solid, fundamental, catholic education, our parish will suffer and some reductions may be necessary. We must continue educating children with no problems, no rumors, no suspicions."

Eunice's heart pounded as she recorded the priest's admonishment. While writing, her mind balked hearing about economics, suburban growth or parish rivalry at a meeting about a ten-year old's suicide. Another ten seconds of silence passed before the staff looked to Sister Carmella, seeking guidance, clarity through emotions and pain.

Everyone respected Sister Carmella's calm, pragmatic approach to whatever she encountered. During lunch recess the boys respected her adjudication of playground balls and strikes. Every teacher trusted her expertise, her wisdom, her ability to keep children's learning and welfare the primary focus. Recognizing her ordained and lay teacher's tensions and anxiety, Sister Carmella composed her mind, her head bobbing back and forth, ever so slightly. Looking first to Father O'Neill, then the others seated along the table, she calmly put her words in order, speaking compassionately, "Sisters, Teachers, our role is to be a resource of hope and faith; a balm for all our little one's sorrows. We will offer prayers for Paulie Keagan and his family. We will be even-tempered in the love of Christ as we complete these last days of our school-year. We will extend every grace to every child; this is what we are called to do."

Some heads nodded in agreement, others remained contemplative, weighing Sister Carmella's words, Father O'Neill's focus; measuring both against the monstrosity of Sister Dominic. Father O'Neill then stood up and nodding quickly, left without saying another word. As others quietly left in twos and threes, Eunice returned the notepad to her desk. The meeting was over at 5:10 P.M., dinner wouldn't be too late.

******

With the table pulled away from the wall, the Daugherty family gathered around in the small, temperate kitchen. Meals were a time of close physical proximity; Martin at the head, an arm's length from the telephone mounted on the wall. At the opposite end, Eunice took her place with Mary Rose seated close to her right. Mark James sat to Eunice's left, his back against the wall, while Michael being the oldest, enjoyed the favor of sitting to his father's left.

Their one and one-half story house on Hosmer Street, was little more than a mile from St. Philomena's. A simple main floor plan of living room, kitchen, two bedrooms, bathroom, hallway and front closet. Upstairs, a loft with two dormer windows faced the street with two closets and twin beds for Michael and Mark James. The basement kept Martin's work bench, Mary Rose's kitchen set and play area with a rug large enough for kneeling football or basketball. Handmade shelves kept luggage, Christmas ornaments, extra bedding and Eunice's canned vegetables behind old curtains. Ten years ago, the housed felt more than adequate, comfortable. Now, with a growing eighth-grader, a sixth-grader and a fourth-grader, the once charming nest was cramped.

Eunice devoted herself to making sure her children were fed, clean and happy every day. She took employment at St. Philomena's as receptionist, general secretary and coordinator of students dispatched for appointments or receiving forgotten lunches. Her salary of forty-four dollars a week bought family groceries, paid for field trips, shoes and occasionally yarn and knitting needles for Eunice. After the children went to bed, she would knit in the living room while Martin watched the home's only television. Married almost seventeen years, Eunice was grateful. She had a home, three beautiful children, a college-educated husband who worked at a major accounting firm, a newer Chevrolet Biscayne and almost ten-thousand dollars in savings. She was thirty-eight years old and her life evolved over the years into a safe, stable, happy existence watching those she loved grow and mature.

Dinner started as usual, Martin asked boys about school; was Michael going to play summer baseball? What about Mark James? Now old enough, would he try out for Pony League? Michael nodded, his mouth full of Eunice's coveted meatloaf and gravy. Mark James scooped some mashed potatoes onto his fork before eagerly stabbing his meatloaf slab. Bringing his fork up, preparing to swallow the mound whole, he asked aloud, "Hey, did you hear about that kid at school? Paulie Keagan?"

Eunice dropped her fork, it clanked off her plate's edge, hit the table and then spun down to the linoleum floor. Mary Rose's head popped up as she stiffened, her face pale. Martin picked up his plastic tumbler of water, "What about him?"

"I heard he died" Michael offered.

"No, I mean yeah, he died. I heard he hung himself in his closet," Mark James' eyes were wide, "Jimmy Buscemi's dad went there, got him out of the closet."

"Really?" Martin and Michael chimed in unison.

"Boys, no more," Eunice said, reaching down for her fork.

"Yeah, Jimmy said his mom found him." Mark James continued, "Can you imagine? Finding your kid hanged in his closet?"

Mary Rose's face crumpled into its center, eyes tightly shut, her nostrils flared white, one hand clenched her fork, she sat back as her cry climbed up through her potatoes and green beans, a small dab of the mixture falling onto her lap.

"I SAID NO MORE!" Eunice's body shook as her grimace slammed the table talk.

Everyone sat motionless, frozen by her maternal roar's intensity, forceful, final. Even Mary Rose, red and teary-eyed, stopped her emotional collapse. Martin slowly moved his palms down to his thighs, fingers pointed inward. A moment later as he watched his mother, Michael resumed chewing slowly, one mandible rotation at a time.

His forearms on the table's edge, Mark James leaned, fixed as a photograph. Seeing her family's shock as her words echoed off kitchen surfaces, Eunice looked to each child, trying to control the fury in her heart, her confusing agony and guilt running amok, churning her stomach. She looked to each, one by one, their images blurring her last memory of Paulie Keagan Junior.

She wondered what was her friend Patricia Keagan doing that moment? Was she finishing dinner? Did she even have dinner?

How could she make dinner when her child was dead? As these thoughts and emotions jousted through her, she felt the kitchen area slowly swirling, off balance, dystopic. She leaned forward, putting her elbows on the table, something no one was ever allowed, bringing her fingers together, weaving them as her index fingers and thumbs caught her forehead. Her eyes down, as her tears formed, she announced, "The child of my friend, my daughter's classmate, has died. There'll be no talk at this table like it's a sports event. We'll respect the family. We will not gossip; we will pray for Paulie and his family.

Martin and the boys solemnly nodded. Eunice peered to the other end of the table under her hands' visor, only then did she detect Mary Rose's shaking, only then did she consider her daughter's grief.

"Mary honey," Eunice reached out to Mary's shoulder. The little girl looked to her mother as her despair found voice. Her mouth opened silently to display all her food as Eunice softly prodded, "finish your bite sweetie, you don't want to choke."

Nodding obediently through glassy eyes, Mary Rose closed her lips, chewed three times and swallowed, her right hand still clutching the fork so tightly her knuckles were white. Seeing Mary Rose's pain, Eunice put the dinner, the evening, the world, on hold; focusing completely on her ten-year old. Extending her hand softly to the child's crown she asked, "Was Paulie a friend of yours, sweetie?"

Still focused on her mother's face, the little brunette head bobbed up and down. With clear throat and clean heart, she replied, "He sits behind me."

"Oh? What's he like?" Eunice hoped a fond memory would ease the moment.

"He's nice, doesn't talk much." Mary Rose looked to the wall behind Mark James, "Sister Dominic doesn't like him."

The air now began condensing again, bringing the room back to a smaller, more humid setting. Martin asked his daughter, "What makes you say that pumpkin?"

"She hits him. A lot."

Martin looked to Eunice, his face snarled in disgust. Eunice looked to her sons, first Michael then Mark James, both avoided her eyes; instant confirmation their sister told the truth. Never in her life did Eunice think her children could be at risk in a classroom. Looking to Mary Rose, Eunice cautiously asked, "Honey, did anything happen this week? Between Sister Dominic and Paulie?"

Mary Rose extended her hand to the table, released her fork and stared at the remnants of her meal. Her brain was churning, the thumb of her left hand softly tapping against the table. Blinking once, twice, a third time, she took a deep breath. Eunice prompted, "Honey, if something happened that bothers you, please tell me, I want to help you."

The family waited silently, watching their smallest one struggle under the weight of something never encountered before. Fifteen seconds bore on Eunice like fifty pounds before Mary Rose bowed her head and spoke to her lap, "Paulie's milk spoiled."

"What?"

"Monday," the soft, little voice resigned flatly, "Last Friday he forgot his lunchbox. Left it in the coat closet. Sister made him drink it, in front of us."

Eunice was dumbstruck, she looked to Martin, equally stupefied, his eyebrows knitted as he brought his hand to his mouth while leaning forward on the table. Eunice followed, "Made him drink it? Why?"

With another sigh, Mary Rose reported, "she said it was a sin to waste food. A sin to be stupid and forgetful. She made him drink the whole thermos, in front of us."

Tears started filling Mary Rose's eyes. Eunice looked to her sons, tears forming in Mark James' eyes, Michael's jaw clenched, nostrils white, his stare flaming back. Mary Rose blurted through her sorrow, "Paulie went to his desk. Then, he threw up, all over the floor!"

Eunice suddenly remembered Anthony Broglio, a fifth-grader, coming to the office and requesting the janitor come to Room 12, saying 'a kid in our class got sick.'

Looking to Mary Rose, Eunice cautiously asked, "Mary, honey, did Sister Dominic help Paulie when he got sick?"

Staring down into her lap still, Mary Rose closed her eyes, her face tightened, tears streaming freely, "No. She said that's what happens to children who waste their lunch. Jesus doesn't love children who waste food."

Eunice's stomach knotted in revulsion and disgust. Two hours earlier she sat just twelve feet from the woman who criticized and dismissed a ten-year old suicide victim. Fighting to remain calm, watching her daughter struggling to collect every molecule of her strength, Eunice focused her entire being on comforting her daughter.

"Honey, Jesus loves everyone. He loves Paulie Keagan, I'm sure."

Mary Rose looked up to her mother, "Sister Dominic says Jesus doesn't have to love us; he chooses who to love. We have to pray Jesus will love us. Because we're sinners, we have to pray."

"Well, we do have to pray. And we should pray for everyone that's true."

"BUT I PRAYED FOR PAULIE, EVERY DAY!" Mary's outrage overwhelmed her, fueling more tears. "Every day, Sister tells him he's stupid. I prayed Jesus would help Paulie. I prayed for

Sister to leave him alone. I asked Jesus to make Sister like Paulie, like she likes me. I prayed to Jesus for Paulie every day! Now he's dead!"

Mary Rose sat back, crushed under the weight of religious doctrine, confusion and grief. Her body shook, her inconsolable sobs offered up groans, mumbled pleas for relief. Eunice looked directly to Martin, shaking her head side to side, words and emotions crashing about her mind. Recognizing the moment, Martin rose from his chair and went through the narrow lane behind Michael to scoop up his sobbing daughter, exhausted by her revelations. Lifting her gently to his chest, with the balance of a wire-walker, he worked his way out of the kitchen to his living room chair, softly, gently carrying Mary Rose.

Eunice watched her husband carry their child in the peace and strength of his embrace to the living rooms' soft evening shadows. She gazed at the serving dishes, empty plates, glasses, salt and pepper shakers, all so innocuous thirty-minutes ago. Tonight, her house was invaded by tears and a rude awakening of horrible events that challenged her beliefs about schools, teachers and faith. Looking to Michael and Mark James, Eunice commanded, "Boys, help me clear the table."

Without objections, the two brothers rose and silently began working, anticipating their mother's every move. Emptying trash, washing and drying dishes, putting everything away, was all completed without words or conflict. No one wanted to go in the living room. No one wanted to see the exhausted child sleeping in her father's protection. Neither boy wanted to consider what suicide meant to a family. At 7:30, Eunice pulled Mary Rose from Martin's lap, softly cooing, "C'mon precious baby, time for bed."

Mary Rose never moved, never opened her eyes. Sleep was her deep escape, her mind and soul's respite to sort emotions, fears and confusion. Martin turned on the television, diffusing his stress through network programming. Keeping the volume low, he sat in the picture tube's gray-white glow. Eunice sat by Mary Rose's bed, the short Cinderella table lamp's 15-watt vigilance guarding the small bedroom.

Changing into her nightgown, Eunice came to the living room, kissed Martin goodnight and went to bed. In the darkness, she lay trying to sort the days' events, hour by hour, minute by minute. Never before had she witnessed such callous and insensitive behavior by a nun. She'd grown up in an Irish-Catholic household where priest's and nun's authority were never questioned. In college she encountered opinions that challenged catholic dogmas and doctrines, which only reinforced her devotion. Tonight, she couldn't sleep knowing her daughter witnessed physical, verbal and spiritual abuse. How many times? How bad was it? Why didn't anybody say anything?

Broken Windows, Renovated Souls

******

Thursday morning, the Daugherty's all dutifully shuffled into St. Philomena's, respectfully, quietly at 8:00 A.M. Michael, Mark James and Mary Rose obediently sat on the chairs outside the office as Eunice unlocked the door and went to her desk. Ten minutes later, Michael spied Sister Beatrice standing by the swings and rallied his brother and sister as he called, "Mom, we're going outside."

"Okay" called back from the office. Mark James' quickly deposited three lunches on Eunice's desk before he tore out of the office to catch up.

Eunice retrieved her steno notepad with Wednesday's meeting minutes. Propping it upright; in placard-like presentation, she took off the Royal typewriter shroud, then took sheets of blank paper out of her drawer. Inserting a page while rolling the carriage, she lined up the edges and corners before snapping the roller into place. Setting her fingertips to the keys, she eyed the waiting pad, but before her first keystroke, Father O'Neill entered the office with Sister Carmella Rose behind him.

"Oh, Mrs. Daugherty, you're here. Good. Would you join us please?" The priest looked to her desk, typewriter and steno pad "Are those the minutes from last night's meeting?"

Eunice nodded.

"Good," Father O'Neill replied, "Would you bring them with you?"

As Father O'Neill spoke, Sister Carmella unlocked her office door and opened it, switching on the light before going to her desk. Father O'Neill entered and pulled the single chair in front of the desk to his right. Although not yet 8:15, the office was warm from the morning sun's glare coming through the windows. "Sister, can you close the blinds please, we don't need all this, brightness."

Sister Carmella stepped to the chords at the window's left edge and smoothly pulled, watching the vertical panels slide to her right, slowly rotating, quietly dimming the room. Eunice came in and seeing nowhere to sit, went back out to the lobby.

Returning with a chair, she saw Father O'Neill's hand motion to close the office door. Setting the chair before the desk, Eunice dutifully walked to the door and closed it. She returned to her seat, steno pad in hand, looking first to Sister Carmella, then to Father O'Neill. The room was quiet, an awkward silence amongst the three adults. Sister Carmella asked Eunice, "Mrs. Daugherty, I, we, wanted to talk to you about yesterday's meeting. Have you typed up the minutes yet?"

"No sister, I was just about to."

Father O'Neill asked, "Are those your notes, the minutes, there in your hand?"

"Yes father, I was just starting."

"There's no need Mrs. Daugherty," he interrupted, "If you would just give them to me, that'll be enough." The father extended his hand, palm up, waiting for Eunice to hand over the notepad. Her face opened, her eyes searching, "But, I haven't typed them yet."

Sister Carmella, in her even, somewhat dour voice replied, "Mrs. Daugherty, we must insist you keep yesterday's meeting, statements, strictly confidential."

"Confidential?"

"Yes," the sister continued, "this is strictly a church matter. It needn't bother the teachers or parents, or the community."

"But a student died," Eunice stammered, "wha-what about his family?"

"Yes, that's unfortunate, but no one knows when Satan may strike us. Right now, we must be strong for St. Philomena's, the church, our staff," attempting to smile, Sister Carmella added, "and the Keagan's of course."

Shock began numbing Eunice, she felt herself shrinking, the

chair seat sagging, the room closing around her, was she really hearing these words? Father O'Neill furthered pressed, "We must be strong for the Keagan's too, yes. But there are those outside the faith, looking for any opportunity to attack or smear St. Philomena's, the Roman-Catholic church, even our most holy father Pope John. We must always be mindful of Satan's constant war against us. Events like this cannot deter our faith."

Hearing the priest speak, Eunice thought, *'I sat across from the evil, it didn't look like Satan to me.'*

With another slight wave of his hand, his face revealed annoyance at being questioned. Slowly, reluctantly, Eunice rose and taking two steps, delivered the notepad to the seated priest. Returning to her chair, Eunice sat in silence with the other two. After a moment, Eunice calmly asked, "What about Sister Dominic James' class?"

"Father Devine has spoken with Mr. Geahaghan at the funeral home. Little Paulie's memory cards will be available to all students. They will say he was taken from us in the night. I'll offer a special prayer for his soul this Sunday at Mass."

"And Sister Dominic James, what about her?" Eunice bravely queried.

"She's being recalled to the Archdiocese offices in Arlington Heights," the priest answered firmly, his patience strained, "Her talents will be quite useful there." As Father O'Neill stood up, Sister Carmella quickly added, "We will finish our school year and move on from this sad time."

Father O'Neill smiled quickly to both women before opening the door and walking out. After the priest walked away, Eunice turned to see Sister Carmella, biting her lip, her eyes moist. Shaken, Eunice felt betrayed, unable to remain composed, she quickly stood and walked out of the office, down the hall past the teacher's lounge to the Ladies Restroom. Once seated in a stall, she relieved her bladder as her heart sank. Covering her nose and mouth, she stuffed her crying into her hands. Multiple gushes of pain mixed with disgust pushed past her lips into her palms as she clamped down any sounds, fearing once released, sobs would grow to howls, wails of despair, a mother's heartbreak fully unleashed.

Suddenly, the door swooshed open as two women entered the lavatory. Eunice gulped down her almost scream, freezing motionless on the toilet.Her hands smothering her nose and mouth as she listened intently.

"I told Nick, were not staying here. Not after this." It was Mary Thanikos, her words punctuated by her high heels striking the terrazzo floor. A second woman followed, not responding. Eunice sat still, listening intently as she heard water start flowing into a sink.

"What does he think?" Eunice recognized Delores Roberts' question.

"I told him I wanted to move to Hawthorne Woods, you know? We went there last Sunday and looked at the models." The running water splashed about the basin, changing tones and echoes.

"How is it?"

"Very nice." The flowing water stopped and a second later, the sound of the paper towel dispenser rolling out sheets barked across the room. "They've got four different floor plans; one I really like, a split level with four bedrooms."

"Four bedrooms?"

"Uh-huh, they have financing available through Homecrest Financial. Twenty-year mortgage at four and a half percent." The sound of the paper, being worked over hands, wrapped around, crushed, spoke up.

"Twenty years? That's a long time, how much are the houses?"

The split-level is Twenty-one thousand, that's with carpeting, stove and wall oven, and second bathroom for the kids."

"Twenty-one thousand!" Delores objected, "Mary, that's a lot of money."

"Not for my kids, plus one bedroom could be for guests, you know, when family visits. And it's ten minutes from Our Lady of Peace."

Eunice collected herself, stood up in the stall, straightened her dress and stepped out to the counter where both teachers examined themselves in the mirror, Mary Thanikos gently reapplying her lipstick.

"Hello Mrs. Roberts, Mrs. Thanikos," Eunice politely offered.

"Good morning, Mrs. Daugherty," Mary Thanikos replied as she examined her crimson lips, "How are you this morning?"

Delores Roberts looked through the reflection back to Eunice before she plucked her hair, carefully managing her shorter blond curls. As the two women reviewed their appearance, Eunice stepped to an open sink and began washing her hands. Mary Thanikos turned left and with one hand leaned on the counter, "Mrs. Daugherty, have you heard how Mrs. Keagan is doing?"

Eunice stopped washing and reached for a paper towel, "I haven't spoken with her, I'm sure she's devastated."

Peering over Mrs. Thanikos shoulder, Mrs. Roberts asked, "How many children does she have?"

They have one other, a little girl, three years old."

"Any plans for more children?" Delores innocently asked.

"Oh no!" Eunice gulped. Realizing her reaction's strength, she paused, collecting her emotions. Wiping her hands, she looked to the teachers, almost apologetically she replied, "Two years ago Patricia was diagnosed with uterine cancer. She had a hysterectomy. She can't have any more children."

Mary Thanikos staggered, her body shifting under Eunice's words. Delores Roberts' eyes dropped to the floor as she turned back to the mirror. Eunice watched the two women search their minds, mortified by her friend's misfortune yet, grateful for their healthy families. After a moment, Mary looked to Eunice, "If you should speak to Mrs. Keagan, please give her our deepest condolences".

Delores nodded in silent agreement before turning to the door. The two women left Eunice standing at the counter, school children walking through the hallway outside. Thursday began like so many before, children learning, playing, living. Eunice Daugherty worked at her desk, answering the phone, taking a supplies inventory, preparing final report cards for teacher's signatures. All the while she thought of Patricia Keagan, Mary Rose crying at the dinner table, Father O'Neill's dispassionate 'special prayer'.

As the day wore on, Eunice's soul churned, her mind distracted, unfocused, an inner tension built to a feral, almost savage rage. To stabilize her emotions, she left the school at lunch time, walking three blocks to a shopping center where the Woolworth's lunch counter offered a tasty Monte Christo sandwich and fries. Twice she used the pay phone hanging on the wall next to the store front windows. Each conversation was short, no more than two minutes, the second call was to Martin. Once she confirmed he would be home at his usual time, she told him they needed to meet before dinner. "Oh, you'll need to get dinner tonight, after we talk," she instructed, "I'm ordering a large pizza from Connie's, with all the stuff the kids like."

"On Thursday?"

"Hm-hmm. Gotta go, see you tonight. Love you." Eunice returned to the counter where her sandwich and fries awaited. That afternoon, she cleared her desk of her pictures, the pencil can, straightening everything neatly before walking out promptly at 3:30.

******

Martin Daugherty warily entered his house through the side door off the driveway at 5:15 P.M. He entered slowly, cautiously, his eyes searching as he stepped lightly through the empty kitchen to the living room. Standing at the foot of the stairs, he looked into the living room to see his three children watching television. Taking one step forward he asked, "Where's your mother?"

No one blinked, staring fixedly at the screen. Michael, sitting in Martin's chair, answered, "She's in your bedroom, waiting for you."

Martin was perplexed, his wife waiting for him in the bedroom, during daylight hours, was completely unexpected. He continued cautiously to the closed dark oak door. Pushing it open about three inches, he saw Eunice, sitting in her chair, still dressed, her legs crossed, holding a bottle of beer on her knee. Knowing it too late to retreat, he entered the bedroom, "Hey, what's going on?"

"I've made a decision we have to make."

"A decision?"

"Marty, they're covering it up."

"They? Covering up what?"

Eunice took her final swig of beer before placing the empty bottle on her dresser. "That nun abused Paulie Keagan. They're sending her to Arlington Heights, covering it up."

Martin's eyes widened as he processed Eunice's claim. Thinking slowly, he considered alternative explanations, "Maybe she asked to go to Arlington Heights."

"They don't have enough teacher's now Marty. Why would they let one leave? No. They're covering up her abuse of Paulie Keagan."

"Abuse? Who said anything about abuse?" Marty turned to the door, making certain it was closed before stepping to the edge of their bed, closer to Eunice as he took off his jacket.

"You heard your daughter, didn't you? You heard her say that nun hit Paulie, a lot."

Martin stood still, he knew when Eunice's anger was fully stoked it was far safer to let her speak and suffer the storm. He waited a moment, then believing it safe he asked, "And?"

"Our children aren't safe there."

"Aren't safe, whad'ya mean they aren't safe?"

"Do we know these people, Marty? Do we really know them?" Eunice brought her hands to her temples, sifting her hair through her fingers before interlocking them behind her head.

"Every day, we give our children to these people, we hand them over, never thinking a moment about what happens in the classrooms. They come home, we ask about their day, but they don't tell us everything. We assume they're good people because they know our prayers.   Others like them taught us, remember? Remember the things we saw in catholic school, lived through?"

Marty loosened his tie, sat down on the bed and began untying his shoes, letting the laces fall freely. Bending forward slightly, one hand on his knee, he ran the other over his receding hairline. While looking to the floor, he professed, "Eunice, the church knows what's best for children and families."

"Really Marty?" Her hands came back to her lap, she purposely straightened her skirt before asking, "Is that what you tell yourself when you buy your rubbers over in Fairfield?"

His head snapped up, eyes focusing directly on hers, wide at her audacity. Eunice didn't blink, she had four older brothers; when it came to her children, she wouldn't be intimidated.

"Remember when we found out I was pregnant?" She sat erect, composed, legs still crossed at the knee, hands neatly folded over the top kneecap. "We agreed you'd finish college, get your degree. We got married, then lost Martin John."

Eunice again looked out the window, reflecting past sorrow against the evening sky. "I wanted to be a teacher, but we had hospital bills. You were studying for your CPA, so I kept working, answering phones at the insurance agency, taking payments, remember? You said one day I could go back, get my teaching certificate."

Martin nodded, acknowledging a promise stored away, forgotten by paying bills, getting through adult life.

"I wanted a career _and_ a family for my life," Eunice confessed to the window pane. Watching light wisps of clouds softly float above all she knew, Eunice admitted aloud, "I never thought my family would _become_ my career."

Eunice turned to her husband, also looking to the window, lost in memories just as tender. Eunice's smile lightened the mood,

"That was sixteen years ago Marty, … a miscarriage and three children later, here we are."

Martin relaxed a bit before Eunice's question caught him flat-footed, "How much do you make a year Marty?"

"Why?"

"Just answer me, please."

"Including my bonus, Ten-thousand five-hundred."

Eunice was stunned, that was far beyond what she guessed. She kept her composure, letting silence hang between them, slowly nodding her head.

"And I earn Seventeen-hundred at the school." Still nodding, her gaze went back out the window, "That's over twelve thousand between us Marty."

"Eunice, what are you getting at?"

"I look at my boys and have little fear. They see their futures in you, successful, married, happy, safe."

Placing both feet on the floor, Eunice leaned forward, her forearms atop her thighs, hands past her knees, fingers locked together. Her face somber, voice soft, her words deliberate, "But, what does Mary Rose see in me? What can she expect when she's grown?"

Eunice looked to her husband, caught in the process of mental awakening. Staring to Marty, Eunice softly, sincerely, pleaded, "I want more for her, more than being at the mercy of whatever life delivers. I want her strong like Michael, self-confident like Mark James. She can't feel invalid from making mistakes. I don't want her afraid of what some stranger might do to her in the name of Jesus."

Eunice watched her words move through Martin's ears and mind, down to his heart. Recognizing his wife's truth, he looked to her with curious eyes. Eunice reinforced her voice, "I want us to move Marty, to Hawthorne Woods. Now."

"Hawthorne Woods? You know how expensive it is?"

Eunice leaned forward, hands clasping her knees, "Yes, I do. We can afford it."

"Why should we leave? We're happy here, the kids are happy here. Because of this Paulie Keagan thing?" Trying to be rational, Martin's reluctance only stoked Eunice's coals.

"Don't patronize me, Martin John!" She stood up and walking three paces, started unbuttoning her dress. Opening the closet, she stepped out of the dress and reached for a hangar. Next her slip came off, then her shoes. Martin watched, still entranced by his wife's figure. Eunice had no thoughts of romance or affection, instead her soul declared the essence of Eunice Marie Deagnan Daugherty.

"Children are life's most precious gift Marty; our only connection to the future. We watch them grow, hoping, praying they'll get every chance for a full, happy life. How can we justify delivering them to strangers who've never been parent's themselves?"

Martin listened intently as Eunice continued, "The world is scary enough Marty, do we want to risk our children at a school where they're considered a means of income? I'd rather have one of my arms cut off, than let them harm a hair on my child's head."

Slipping on her cut-off shorts, Eunice searched a drawer for a top. Pulling one over her head, she guided the supple fabric down her torso, letting it hang loosely.

"Eunice," Martin objected, "We can't afford a bigger house, the furniture, what about the kid's college money? Have you thought about that?

"What do you work for Marty? Why are we here? What's most important in our lives? A bank account? A new car? What? Our children give us meaning before they grow up and grow away. We're selling this house Martin. I called Rosalynn Hayes, the realtor, she's coming Saturday to list our house. OUR children deserve all we can give them, however we give it and by Jesus Christ almighty, if I have to work three jobs, I will!"

Taking the doorknob in hand, Eunice gripped it almost as firmly as her conviction. Thinking for a moment, she then turned and went back to the nightstand on her side of the bed. She lifted up the small, white book laying under the lamp. Thumbing pages quickly, she scanned the correct spot. Putting her finger between the pages, she looked to her husband, who was changing his clothes.

"I've never asked for much before, and truthfully, I'm not asking now." Her eyes focused as he pulled his jeans up to snap the fly buttons into their eyelets. Waiting a moment to regain Marty's attention, Eunice held her fire. When his eyes met hers, the scriptural fusillade began, "It says it right here, *'And Jesus said, 'Whoever receives one such child in My name receives Me, but; whoever causes one of these little ones who believe in Me to stumble, it would be better for him to have a heavy millstone around his neck, and to be drowned in the depth of the sea.'*

Eunice looked directly into Martin's eyes, "I will not look away Marty, I will not let others harm any child, ours or anyone else's. I would rather have that millstone around my neck than let our children suffer from these people."

"Eunice, you're overreacting," Marty explained, "Our children are fine."

"Are they Marty? Are they?" she snapped. Her jaw set, with focused glare and just cause, she kept firing, "Maybe tomorrow, but what about next year? When Michael's in high school with, God knows who, and we're still at St. Philomena's?"

Eunice watched Marty thinking, unresponsive. She waited for his objection. Sensing no reply, she narrowed her focus and in low voice averred, "I don't know what you're thinking Martin John Daugherty, but know this. If we don't move to Hawthorne Woods, those rubbers in your drawer will turn to dust before you get close to me again."

Husband and wife stood two feet apart, tension locking each, their feet and positions fixed. The time to agree clicked from Martin's alarm clock; click, click, click, click. Neither batted an eye, each one's breathing barely detectable. The accountant's mind scrambled calculating costs, expenses, the work involved in moving: the mother's ferocity piercing through determined eyes; her decision made. Then Martin blinked, stepping back, he put hands on his hips, "Did you order the pizza?"

Eunice's eyes softened, her ingénue smile emerged as she leaned to his chest, putting her hand over his heart, "I told them you'd pick it up at six o'clock. What time is it?"

"Ten to six."

"Ooh, you'd better get going."

Thirty-five minutes later, grace was said as the steaming entre waited in the kitchen table's center. Three hungry children salivated through every phrase all the way to, 'Amen.' Then three arms of varying length surged to the hot pizza, pulling and jerking pieces onto paper plates. Both parents patiently waited until the first attack ended. Taking their pieces, each lifted a beer bottle in silent toast, watching their children and smiling, blessed, safe. As warm, setting sunlight poured into the small kitchen, Eunice asked, "Guess what?"

Three faces looked up, first to her, then Martin, then back to Eunice, innocent faces of fourteen, twelve and ten, politely waiting. Smiling broadly Eunice announced, "On Saturday, you all need to start cleaning out your rooms and closets."

"AAWWW!!" Erupted through mouthfuls of pizza, a chorale of alarm and surprise. Michael stopped mid-chew, puzzled. Mark James looked to his brother first then his father. Mary Rose chewing softly, looked to her mother's face, curious, wondering.

"Yes, and we'll need to get empty boxes from the grocery store. Sunday, after Mass, we're going to look for a new house," Eunice beamed across the table.

Martin watched his children turn their heads left and right, back and forth, searching their parent's faces. Elated in her moment, Eunice cooed to her children, "We're getting a bigger house."

"Will we still be together Mommy?" Mary Rose asked, wide eyed, holding her pizza just beyond her lips.

Leaning toward her only daughter, Eunice smiled, "Yes precious, we'll all be together."

"No more St. Philomena's?"

"No honey, no more St. Philomena's." Eunice's love shone warmly, engulfing the small face, its emerald green eyes brightly shining over freckled cheeks and full smile. The mother's green eyes smiled back, "Time to move baby."